SYLVIA'S DREAM

OLERICULTURE

Richard M Beloin MD

authorHOUSE®

AuthorHouse™
1663 Liberty Drive
Bloomington, IN 47403
www.authorhouse.com
Phone: 1 (800) 839-8640

Published by AuthorHouse 05/14/2019

ISBN: 978-1-7283-1213-2 (sc)
ISBN: 978-1-7283-1212-5 (e)

Print information available on the last page.

This book is printed on acid-free paper.

DEDICATION

This book is dedicated to four great friends who helped our transition to the Rio Grande Valley—Milt, Diane, Charlie and Jean.

CONTENTS

BOOK ONE

SYLVIA

CHAPTER 1—The Early Years

Ranching life for the last four generations had not changed much in the methods of raising livestock and being self sufficient on the family ranch. Now this was the fifth generation and changes had come to pass. Gone were the days when a rancher would raise thousands of cattle over the open range and rely on the roundup to properly select, brand and cull the herds of all the surrounding ranchers.

Now this was the fifth generation of Cassidys and in 1884, Grant and Nellie, ages 50 and 49 were the parents of three children. Sylvia age 12, Bryan age 16 and Stan age 22. Stan was married to Wilma and they had a newborn son named Alex.

Ranching had slowly changed in the past five years. The open range was closing down. Oil was driving companies to purchase large tracks of land in hopes of finding oil. This in turn was forcing ranchers to fence in their land to secure their borders from the encroaching oil fields. The drought also contributed to changes. The Cassidy ranch, the BAR C BAR Ranch (--C--), was spread out over eight sections. Each section was a square mile or 640 acres. Therefore, the ranch covered some five thousand acres. Because of it's limits, the ranch acreage could only hold a thousand head of cattle. With the drought, the herd size was decreasing by the seasons as lack of forage was naturally culling the herd with non-thriving livestock that had to be sold at below normal prices.

It was in the mid 1880's that Grant and Nellie saw the potential of expanding their hobby of growing food into a secondary business that allowed diversification of their land. Since, for hundreds of years people grew their own food, and expanding a labor of love into an income producing benefit was easily accepted by Sylvia and Bryan. So, over the next few years, the backyard garden grew into a going enterprise under the guidance of Grant, Nellie, Sylvia and Brian. Stan was not interested in the agriculture component and stayed on the range taking care of cattle with two of his cowhands.

The first thing that Grant did was dig for water. Fortunately, water wells were producing a sufficient amount of water to maintain a holding pond of water for each windmill well. With an investment of six windmill wells, the Cassidy family started cultivating land for planting. Every plot of land was tied to one holding pond where the planting took place in each well's flood plain. Grant went ahead and with the drought related culling, he took the money and bought equipment. He purchased a two-way plow, a disc harrow and a finish harrow. All with the operator sitting on the cultivators and behind a team of work horses—no more walking behind a horse.

Over the next several years, the gardens grew, and the self-sustaining private garden grew into a "truck farm"—an operation where vegetables were grown for market. Grant designed a special vegetable wagon with bins and display cases all protected with a roof against sun and rain. This wagon served to transport their vegetables to Dallas as well as serve as a mobile "bodega" of sorts. In actuality, the wagon was displayed in a "farmer's market" area for vendors to sell their wares.

The fourth year of operations saw a weekly income profit of $30-40. The difficulty looming was the fact that Sylvia, their most enthusiastic worker, was leaving the family business to enter into a one- year program at the University to study Olericulture—the science of growing vegetables for food to include production and marketing. Sylvia made it clear to her family that her future would be working for a large agricultural company as the resident agronomist/olericulturist.

Sylvia finished her local schooling by age sixteen in grade ten. Since she could not enter the University till age 17, she enrolled in the local community college to take courses in botany as preparation for her year at the University. During that year, Sylvia also started experimenting in cross pollinating plants as well as single seed potting for transplanting plugs. The last course she took just before her University program began was the study of bees and their use growing vegetables. In this last course she learned how to build a beehive and a complete apiary of hives. She learned how to extract honey from the hive which would supplement their vegetable crops at market.

By departure time, Sylvia had contributed her ideas and hard work to develop the Cassidy vegetable brand, --C-- (or the Bar C Bar brand or trademark). What she did not know was what would happen to the vegetable business once she was gone. Her dad had already hired a middle-aged couple as Sylvia's replacement. Even without the college certificate, Sylvia knew that the limitation, to growing the vegetable business, was a single growing season—not conducive to building a commercial year-round business!

***

Sylvia arrived at the University on Sept. 1, 1889. This was a one- year course that finished Aug. 31, 1890. Unlike the academic schedule, this was truly a twelve-month course with plenty of field work during the last three months of the year—June, July and August. There was a two-week vacation at Christmas when the entire school closed. There was also a one-week vacation at Easter, but the school stayed open for those who wished to stay on campus.

Arriving at the registration desk, Sylvia introduced herself and said, "I have a bank voucher for $600 as payment for my course." "Yes, young lady, you have signed up for a totally inclusive one-year course in Olericulture. This fee includes room and board, laundry service, books, implements, work clothes and boots, class and laboratory instruction and field work. Just remember, you need to pay for your personal, hygienic effects and health needs. Plus, you must leave the campus for two weeks at Christmas—either you go home, stay with a friend or stay in a hotel."

"Now, please sign these forms and your guide will take you to your dormitory and finish the registration." Sylvia signed the forms and then turned to meet the dormitory floor manager who took over the conversation. "Hello, Sylvia. I'm Margaret Sullivan, for etiquette purposes, please call me Mrs. Sullivan as I am a widow. Leave your large bags here, and a porter will bring them to your room. The ladies walked directly to Cramer Hall and Mrs. Sullivan talked all the way. My floor is the second floor. I supervise ten rooms of five girls."

"There is a large ten stall toilet and shower for each floor. My room is also the mail room, conference room and private apartment. If you have a problem, please come and see me at my private apartment. The free laundry room is in the cellar and the coffee/tea/water room is next to my room. The coffee room is open 24 hours a day and it's free. Snacks are available at the campus store, to keep in your room, but at your costs. Lights out and quiet time is at 10PM, unless you like to study by candle-light (which is the low intensity setting on your desk lamp). Keep in mind the library is open 24 hours a day."

"The campus cafeteria opens at 6AM for those with 8AM classes and closes at 9AM. Reopens at 11:30AM to 1:30PM, and 5PM to 7PM. Now getting back to my floor, this floor is the agricultural floor. So, any girl on this floor will be seeking an agricultural degree. All agricultural classes, labs and greenhouses are in the Hill building. This school offers 11 different degrees in agriculture. Your certificate will be in Olericulture and here is your schedule of classes, labs and greenhouse times. Now spend the time and meet your four roommates. Be back at the cafeteria for lunch and after lunch I will give you a walking tour of the entire campus. One last thought, the dorm room is where you do your studying and sleeping. The campus is where you date men and do your kissing etc. etc. etc."

Sylvia then entered "room 3" and was immediately greeted by her five new roommates. Introductions followed and Sylvia at least caught their first names: Sally, Jean, Diane, Dixie and Lynn. Diane said, "I'm also taking the one-year course in Olericulture and this is your bed, study desk and closet, next to mine." Sylvia kept talking while unpacking all her clothes. Her desk had a locked drawer for valuables and personals. The traveling bags were placed in the communal overflow closet in the room.

While all the roommates were finishing their unpacking, Sylvia opened her course schedule to see a six-day schedule with Sunday off and extending to the Christmas holiday. The first four months during the fall months were spent in the class room, laboratory and greenhouse. The post-holiday schedule would likely include much more field work!

MWF 8-9:30AM Agronomy—Applied Botany for vegetables.
10-11:30AM Olericulture—Vegetable production.
1-2:30PM Laboratory—watering and insect control.
3-5PM Greenhouse—Preparing potting soils & germination.

TTS 8-9:30AM Agronomy—Soil type for a specific crop.
10-11:30AM Olericulture—Vegetable marketing.
1-2:30PM Laboratory—Mineral analysis and pH.
3-5PM Greenhouse—Pots, tube plugs and transplanting.

As promised, Mrs. Sullivan picked up all the floor girls and lead them to the cafeteria. There were three choices: fruit salad, hot vegetable platter and chicken fricassee. Sylvia took the fruit salad which was rare in their ranch area. Diane took the hot vegetable platter and the other three girls took the fricassee. Diane commented, "there are vegetables and then there are real vegetables!" Sylvia asked what she meant, "these are not just boiled vegetables, these are cooked in such a way that enhances the flavor beyond belief." Sylvia was offered a taste and quickly appreciated the taste difference—a point for the future.

After lunch, Mrs. Sullivan provided the campus tour. Sylvia noted where everything was located but made a specific note of where to find certain buildings she might need: the doctor's office, the library, the book and general store, the church, the security office, the administration building, and of course the Hill building—the Agriculture building.

Since Mrs. Sullivan was touring the girls from the agriculture dormitory floor, she carefully went thru the Hill building--through every floor and every room. The first floor was all classrooms with one large stadium type lecture hall. The second floor was all laboratories to include botany, physics, etymology, chemistry (both qualitative and organic). The third floor was all greenhouses. There were two types: all glass and screened for sun penetration control. The screened ones were for starting plants and the clear glass ones were for plant growth. At the end of the tour, everyone gathered at the cafeteria for dinner. The menu was grilled chicken or meatloaf with a choice of two vegetables. There were several cakes for dessert with plenty of coffee or tea. After dinner, everyone was invited to the first social dance and gathering at the campus social club. It was during this event that Sylvia had an epiphany. She did not socialize much that evening and on their way back to the dorm, Dianne asked why she didn't mingle or even dance.

"While I was watching you dancing and mingling, I came to an illuminating realization. Why am I here? Am I here to get a Mrs. degree or an Agricultural certification or both? Am I looking for a husband to take with me in my future endeavors or to follow him in his chosen future? Can I find time to socialize and develop a relationship, with the anticipated study requirements to get the most out of my courses?"

Diane adds, "I'm here for both. Actually, I think I found the man of my dreams already tonight. I spotted him before the dance started, kept staring at him till he started to stare back. When the music started, he walked over and asked me to dance. I then spent the rest of the evening with him. And that's how quick it can happen."

"Yes, I saw, and it helped me to make up my mind. I want a degree and a professional life. I'm only seventeen and there is plenty of time for falling in love and raising a family. If I can make the career happen, I know the other part of my life will happen. There's a time for everything, and now is the time to get certified with an agricultural degree. I want to leave here with the knowledge that will make me secure with my profession!"

The next day, classes started promptly at 8AM. The morning coffee was having its effect and at the 9:30 break everyone was lining up to use the facilities. After three hours of lectures, it became clear that the entire evening would be spent studying and researching additional facts about the class subject. Fortunately, the class lectures followed the chapters of the two textbooks she had. The hours spent in the lab and greenhouses were also supported in the chapters corresponding to the day's work.

Any further knowledge could only be obtained in the library's agricultural section. Sylvia spent many Sunday afternoons during library research on the subjects mentioned during the week. To match the lecture material, the Olericulture section had reference texts and articles written by the lecturers that expanded on the presented subjects.

The afternoon labs were a new method of teaching for a gal coming from a small country school without scientific labs. She learned applied theory and practical applications for a scientist in the field.

Hours were spent on mineral analysis of nutrients to include nitrogen, potassium, magnesium, phosphorous and other trace minerals. Applying this mineral ratio allowed a proper choice of vegetables that would grow best in this soil. She also learned how to add commercially available minerals per acre to achieve the ideal ratio for planted vegetables.

The significance of soil pH was another revelation. It was a difficult subject to transfer the mathematical theory into a practical application. Knowing that different pH's were needed for maximum production of certain vegetables, it allowed the adjustment of soil pH by adding lime to increase the pH (or decrease the acidity), or ammonium sulfate to decrease the pH (or increase the acidity).

By Christmas time it became clear that testing for soil pH and adjusting the acidity or alkalinity was an easy test to perform in the field and it was something that could be adjusted fairly easily. The testing of soil nutrients required sophisticated equipment and many hours of work. This analysis could best be achieved by sending a soil sample to the University and paying the required fees. That way the results were reliable.

Receiving a soil analysis enabled comparing the mineral content of the soil with the charts of known best ratios for each vegetable.

Usually, it required the addition of nutrients to reach the desired level for each proposed crop. Nitrogen was best added by adding manure. Magnesium was added by adding Epsom Salt, or if the pH was low by adding lime. Potassium was added by adding ocean bed sand known as greensand, kelp meal, ashes (especially hardwood) or used coffee grounds. Phosphorous was added by bone meal or manure. Commercial phosphate was now available because of phosphorous depleted land from overgrazing or harvesting of hay crops.

Sylvia recalled a specific lecture on the do's and don'ts of using manure. Fresh manure had such a high content of nitrogen and ammonia that its use could harm plant growth. Manure from cows, horses and chickens all needed to stay inactive in the manure pile for one year to allow the manure to compost, cure and degrade. Then a thinly applied layer of one-year old manure at the rate to 10-30 pounds per 100 sq. ft. would then be cultivated into the soil during fall months to allow the soil to remain dormant during the winter months.

Chicken manure provided an advantage to vegetable growers because it was not only a great source of nitrogen and phosphorous, but chickens provided a great source of fresh farm eggs that always complimented any vegetable stand. In addition, chickens were a great source of meat to the vegetable farmer.

The greenhouse training was a new idea that the University was promoting. Sylvia was intrigued by the two types of houses used—shade and full glass. The shade type was a house surrounded and covered with a semi-transparent screen/mesh that allowed air and partial sun to enter. This house was used to prepare potting soils and planting of individual seeds in tubes or pots. Sylvia had no idea how involved this process could be.

To Sylvia's surprise, potting soil had no ground dirt. It was made up of a mixture of: screened plant compost, sand, peat moss, pine bark, perlite (a volcanic rock), sawdust and lime. Solarized garden soil was used because it was a cheap potting soil starter. Being solarized meant that a section of the garden was covered in a sheeting that allowed the sun to cook the earth for 4-6 weeks, to kill weed seeds, insects and pathogens. You could also accomplish the same by placing trays of dirt in large ovens and sterilizing the soil that way.

The greenhouse manuals provided the different potting soil recipes for different vegetables. Once the potting soil was prepared, it was added to one-inch glass tubes. A seed was added and the soil lightly watered. An entire rack of planted glass tubes was then covered till germination occurred. After germination occurred, the plugs were kept in the shade house till the plant hardened and were then transferred to the fully glassed houses. There they were watered and eventually transferred to clay pots to mature before being field planted.

The greenhouse training was a pleasurable hands-on portion of the course. It also allowed a continuum from seed, to transplant, to harvest in the field. The students were told that all these seeded plugs would be transplanted by them into the University gardens by late fall.

The marketing courses provided a dose of reality. Olericulture was a new concept in agriculture. Vegetables were coming into their own. It was a cheap, renewable, filling, and tasty food that basically needed weeding, cultivation, sun and water. With the growth of cities, the backyard gardens were giving way to market places. Sylvia found herself in the burgeoning trade. As one lecturer said, "it's one thing to be a successful grower with a field of mature plants, but if you don't have a market for them, you have nothing."

So, it was up to the Olericulturist to match the harvest with the proven and guaranteed market. The courses explained how to secure new clients in stores and food distribution centers. Sylvia learned how to set up business contracts and set prices for the goods. It also guided a person in setting up their own business as a mobile unit or a fixed store.

But how to place into practice this accumulated knowledge. Sylvia realized that she had to develop her own crops and marketplace or go to work for a large commercial grower as in the vegetable fields of South Florida or South California. This dilemma would bring her to a long family discussion during the Xmas Holiday.

Meanwhile, it was crunch time since the final exams were around the corner. Each student had to pass all three categories of instruction" the lecture series, the laboratory and greenhouse experience and essays on olericulture. After weeks of late-night studies, the exam days arrived. The first day was on the lecture series. A series of 100 multiple choice questions, followed by an essay on how to establish a commercial vegetable enterprise in a dry land with a low rainfall. The final essay was a description on how to develop a market for your products and make a profit in the process.

Sylvia managed to get through the first day without too much stress. The second day of testing was a real challenge. There was only one question or task: "Build a potting soil with at least seven ingredients or more, an exact pH of 6.0 and a mineral content of Nitrogen 10%, phosphorous 10%, potassium 8%, magnesium 6% and calcium 3%. Once the ratios were finalized convert your recipe to a 25 lb. of potting mix. We were given all day to successfully complete the batch of commercial potting soil. Sylvia completed the recipe an hour before the closing time. Plus, she knew she had nailed it!

Awaiting the corrected exams, everyone knew that you needed a score of 70 to pass and to move to the course's second and final stage. This stage would be 100% field experience and would cover plot cultivation and preparation, soil testing, fertilization and pH stabilizing, transplanting, row planting, irrigation, hand and mechanical plant cultivation, harvest, storage and distribution. This would make you the educated and experienced olericulturist.

The awards ceremony was held for each section separately. Sylvia's event comprised every girl on her floor. Seven students were in the Olericulture section and all seven passed the academic portion. Sylvia took top honors in all categories and went home proud of her work.

***

Meanwhile on the outskirts of Dallas, Grant and Nellie Cassidy were quietly reading after a big lunch. Things in early December were quiet on the Bar C Bar Ranch with the vegetable gardens dormant and the herd still grazing the pastures before the snow arrived. Suddenly, a carriage was heard arriving at the main house. Grant looked out the window and saw a well-dressed business man step onto the porch and knocked at the door. Grant got up to receive him.

"Come in. What can I do for you?"

"May I come in to discuss a very important matter?"

"Certainly, have a seat and can I offer you a glass of fresh lemonade?"

"Well yes and thank you."

"So, what is on your mind."

"I won't beat around the bush. OIL. I work for Humble Oil. The company owns all the land around you, and we are interested in your land."

"Why? Don't you have enough land all around me?"

"Yes, we do. But, is it the right land? Let me explain. Picture a lake of water. On the beaches you have inches of water whereas in the center of the lake you can have hundreds of feet of water. Now picture a lake of oil. On the edges you can have inches of oil and of course a fortune in the center. Now our test holes on the land surrounding you is yielding inches of oil. And where do you think the center of the oil lake might be?"

Nellie says, "Oh my goodness!"

"Yes Mam. We think your eight sections is sitting on a massive lake of oil."

Grant adds, "Theoretically, it sounds good. How do you prove it?"

"With your permission, we would like to dig

a test hole. We may have to dig a few thousand feet, but if we hit oil, you'll know it. Right now, your land is worth 25 cents an acre. If we hit oil, it will be worth $10 an acre and with eight sections of +-5000 acres, it would be worth $50,000 or a combination of cash plus stocks and royalties."

"Them are all big words, how much will it cost us to dig this test well?"

"Nothing, we'll dig it at our cost as long as you sign a promise to deal with us if the well produces and not to deal with any of our competitors."

Grant looks at Nellie. With a nod he says, "where do I sign?"

After the signing, Grant asks for the explanation of the cash alternative.

"Instead of the $50,000. You would receive a royalty of 15% per barrel of crude oil plus 5000 in Humble Oil stocks. At today's value of crude oil as $1 per barrel, that means 15 cents per barrel. By our estimates it would take you twelve years to make up the $50,000 assuming Humble Oil is still in business and your well is also still producing. Clearly, $50,000 cash today with a proper investment would likely double in twelve years. I think that is your best option."

"How about the $50,000 plus 5,000 shares of your Humble Oil stock if the well hits a gusher."

"Yes, for a gusher, I'm certain that can be arranged."

"Good, my daughter, Sylvia, will be home for Christmas and Nellie and I will meet with her, Brian, Stan and his wife Wilma."

"Good, the drilling rigs and crews are now occupied at other oil producing sites. Since digging this well is a speculation, it will likely be months before we get here but I guarantee we'll be here by September 1. The drilling site has been chosen and it is in the center of your land. We'll send you a notice a month ahead of time so you can clear the area of cattle."

***

Sylvia arrived home for the Christmas break by train at the Dallas depot. The entire Cassidy family was there to greet her. Grant had rented a carriage and Sylvia could not stop sharing her many experiences all the way home. After going over all her past four months, she explained what the next eight months would entail. It was Stan who added, "so you are going back to work eight months in the fields at no pay!"

"Actually, I'm paying them for that privilege. I've learned the theory and science, but now I have to put it to real use. The experience will be equal to an apprentice in training. In addition, I have to learn the new implements. We now have a horse drawn potato planter and a harvester. There is a new seeder that can-do line seeding of seeds as small as a carrot seed and it can space them as close as an inch apart. This new seeder is produced by the Moline/Monitor company and is called a grain drill. It consists of a double row of discs that make a furrow. The seeds are then dropped from a top box thru a tube into the furrow. The trailing discs bury the seeds and a roller dampens the soil over the seeds. I need to study and master the settings of these new implements since they are part of all future commercial grower's tools. In addition, new implements are being tested at the University every day."

"What else will you be learning?"

"I'll be learning how to set up row irrigation instead of plot flooding, how to control insects, how to use horse drawn row cultivation and so many other things that will make me a successful grower."

"Does your degree guarantee you a job?"

"No, but the last month is dedicated to preparing a job application, an interview and actually applying at known commercial growers that might be needing the help of a college trained olericulturist. My long- term goal is to have my own enterprise, but that takes capital which I can get from saving as much of my salary as possible."

After unpacking and having a great dinner with the entire family present, Grant took the opportunity to inform them of the arrangement he had made with Humble Oil. He even described the financial options if oil was found on the ranch. After a long period of discussions and questions, Grant asked everyone as to their choices of payment, and their goals for their future off the family ranching homestead. Everyone wanted the $50,000 cash payment with stocks since no one could ever predict when a well would go dry. Or, "a bird in hand is worth more than a hundred on the fly!" In addition, the cash payment would allow each individual to choose his future path. Realizing this benefit, Grant asked the three kids what their plans would be with $10,000 in hand.

Stan was first to answer. "I want out of ranching. I want my own oil drilling rig. I would bank the $10 K and go to work for a well drilling company to learn the ropes. When fully trained, I would use the $10 K to buy a rig and go into private or contracted well drilling."

Wilma looked at everyone and added, "I've heard about his dream since we were married. He is firm in his plans, and I support him 100%."

Grant acknowledged Stan's plans. He then said, "depending on options, your mom and I would probably retire and live in town. What about you Brian?"

"I know what I like and want, but I would rather not declare my wishes until I hear from Sylvia."

"Well Sylvia, you're up."

"During my marketing lectures, the professor pointed out that the country had two major commercial vegetable centers—South California and Florida. These were profitable because they had a year-round growing season. Joining the business in those two areas would be expensive and difficult. He suggested that there is a new area that has not been developed that would provide a year-round growing season."

Brian added, "where is that, Mexico?"

"No, but you are close. It is just north of the Rio Grande river, the Valley as it's called by the local residents. The Valley is a stretch of land that is approximately 35 miles long between two larger communities yet named and extending 20 miles north. It lies +-40 miles west of Brownsville, Texas and some +-120 miles east of Laredo, Texas. The railroad is five years away, but there is shipping via steamers on the Rio Grande from Laredo and Brownsville."

Brian exclaimed, "and it's still in Texas?"

"Yes, and the land is selling for 25 cents an acre. The land is dry and needs irrigation from the Rio Grande. Presently, modified windmills serve as pumps to transfer water from the river to holding ponds for controlled irrigation. Yes, irrigated farming is the wave of the future in this dry land with an average of twenty inches of rain per year."

"Where would you settle in this 30-mile stretch of the "Valley"?

"The large settlement on the west has a population of 600 people and just five miles east is a settlement where land is 25 cents per acre. According to my professor, if you go to the large settlement on the east, adjacent land sells for 50 cents per acre since the railroad will be coming to the valley from Brownsville on the east."

"Historically, this settlement on the Valley's west end started around the Santa Anna Ranch owned by John McAllen. If we were to go investigate, we should start at the ranch and work our way east to find at least one mile of river frontage and a quarter mile extending north into the actual valley. Ideal would be land with a starter house to live in."

Brian could not hold back any longer, "yes, yes, and yes. That's what I want. Sylvia, if you are serious about starting your own enterprise, let's join our moneys and start anew in South Texas. I enjoy driving horses, using cultivating equipment and now new planting implements. I am willing to do most of the heavy work if you are willing to do the planning and marketing."

"Well little brother, if the test well comes in, you have a deal."

Nellie looks at Grant and chimes in, "you all wait a minute, you all know how much your dad and I have enjoyed our little vegetable "truck farm" and we might be interested in joining this venture with the two of you. Let's see if the well comes in before we get the cart before the horse, heh!"

***

Sylvia went back to the University by early January. Schedules were full, from 8AM to 5PM six days a week. Sunday was church day and a time to do library research on subjects discovered during the week. Sylvia worked hard and did her share of the physical work. She enjoyed driving work horses to cultivate and operate new implements. She watched closely as irrigation canals were dug and extended over long tracts of land. There was something new to learn every day.

Without warning, Sylvia received a telegram in late June informing her that Humble Oil would be on site by the 4th of July. The drilling foreman expected it would take two weeks before they could make predictions based on the drilling samples. Sylvia filed the information and continued her work.

Ten days later she received another telegram. This one stated that the drilling samples were showing an ever-increasing amount of oil and other carbon products. She was informed that she should take a leave of absence for the next week because of a family emergency.

Sylvia arrived by train the next day and was picked up by Brian with the ranch buggy. Brian said, "it looks good for a strike any day. Of course, whether it will be a well producing one or one hundred barrels a day still remains to be seen."

"This is all interesting, but why was I called to come home before the well comes in, if it does?"

"Because, if we get a gusher, the oil man representing Humble Oil will want to sign a contract. This would be the last chance for this family to make a final proposal. Dad has been thinking that we might be able to add a small royalty on each barrel of oil over the cash and stock options."

"Oh, this is serious and I'm glad I am here for the showdown."

Two days later the family was at the drill site and were looking at the drilling samples. They looked like an oily mud and the drilling foreman was smiling ear to ear. In addition, the oil man who had made the initial visit with Grant and Nellie was also at the drill site.

Suddenly the earth shook and shuddered. Nellie yells out, "earthquake, hold on." The foreman yells out, "that's not an earthquake Ma'am, that the well about to EXPLODE............AND GUSH." Everyone was looking at the drilling rig and saw a black flume extending hundreds of feet in the sky. Then it started to rain Black Texas Gold. Their helmets kept their hair free of oil, but the rest of their clothes were covered in crude oil. Everyone was dancing and yelling, including the oil man.

It took many hours to cap the high-pressure flume which left a mess of crude oil on the ground. The final stage was the installation of the ground equipment which would extract the oil and store it in capped barrels.

The next day, the oil man arrived. This time he was escorted by two frocked/high-topped well-dressed men carrying briefcases. The Cassidy family was present, and everyone gathered in the family dining room. The oil man finally introduced himself as Winston McMurphy and the two associates were representatives of Bellman and Bellman.

Grant started the discussion. "well Mr. McMurphy we hit a gusher."

"Actually, we hit a super gusher to be exact."

"Well, in that case we need to renegotiate."

Interrupted by the senior Bellman, "well sir, you have already signed a contract regarding payment if the well came in. Why renegotiate?"

"Do you see the word 'super gusher' mentioned in the contract I signed?"

"No, but really...........!"

"So, we need to renegotiate, and I expect you and your associate to shut up. I don't even want you to pass gas till I speak to you again, and if either of you do, you will find yourselves outside."

Mr. McMurphy was smiling as he said, "well, Mr. Cassidy, several months ago you were satisfied with $50,000 and 5000 shares of stock. I am authorized to give you what you want, within reason. What would you want extra?"

"A new offer of cash, stocks and some royalty for each barrel produced."

"Very well, Humble Oil stands to make a bundle from this well and we want it. How about a cash payment of $60,000, 7000 shares of stock and a royalty of 3%? If this well produces 100 barrels a day at the present value of $1 per barrel, you would make $3 a day. That may not seem like a big royalty, but if I'm not mistaken, these 5000 acres will hold several wells at the same production rate. So, if there are four wells producing 400 barrels a day that equals $12 a day or over $4,000 per year. Of course, we dig the wells at our cost. What do you say?"

The Cassidy family moved to the kitchen for a private parley. Grant started by asking, "any thoughts on the subject?

Nellie started by saying, "I say we do it, this is the chance of a lifetime."

Sylvia added, "yes, this is my dream come true."

Brian followed suit. Like Sylvia, I would move to South Texas, so I am in total agreement. Let's do it."

"It's a go for me," Grant added.

The last to vote was Stan. "I agree with you all, time for a change in our lives. Let's do it under two conditions........................"

"Agreed. Let's go back to the dining room."

Back at the dining table, the lawyers looked skeptical that a deal could be reached today. Grant started by saying, "We all accept your final offer under two conditions."

The senior Bellman blurted out his disapproval, "I told you Winston that we were going to be skinned alive."

Winston asked, "what are your two conditions Mr. Cassidy?"

"That we be allowed to sell our cattle and keep the money to buy our next homes."

"Of course, that was always assumed. What is your last condition?"

Bellman again grunted and said, "here it comes!"

"Our last and final condition is that you give Stan a starting and apprentice job on a drilling rig. He wants to join the oil business."

"Done, we have a deal. How long before you plan to move?"

"We will be gone no later than October 1st or sooner. The cattle will be gone, and all the buildings will be empty of animals, implements, furniture and personal belongings."

"Perfect, give the Bellman's an hour to prepare duplicate documents for our signatures and we will be on our way."

Once the documents were signed by all five family members, checks and shares were evenly distributed and issued to the five members. In addition, contracts were individually issued for the yearly royalty checks to all five family members.

The next day, Grant, Sylvia and Brian went to

the bank in Dallas. Stan's check was deposited in his account and his shares were placed in a bank safety deposit box. Bank accounts were started for Sylvia and Brian. The remainder of the checks were then deposited, and everyone had his own safety deposit box for the stock shares.

The next day, Sylvia went back to school. She had the entire month of August as an elective. Since she didn't need to look for a job, she concentrated her efforts into getting ready to be a business owner. She took a quick course in accounting to keep proper business books. She spent a full day at the factory that produced shade and glass greenhouses. She prepared an invoice of the items she would need in South Texas and could activate this order by a telegram. It included a bank transfer of funds by telegram.

Sylvia visited several machinery companies around Dallas and even prepared invoices for implements she would need and would pay also by bank transfer telegrams. With all the orders she was preparing, she paid a deposit of 10% by bank voucher under her account's name. With the professor's help, she made a list of the many items that she would need for field work that she did not have on the homestead in Dallas. It included items from a shade house to crop storage.

Sylvia realized that select items and household furniture would come from central Texas by train to Laredo. There they would travel down the Rio Grande to the ports in the Valley. After getting established in the area, they would rely on the local merchants and freight companies to obtain their necessary goods.

While Sylvia was finishing her year, Grant and Brian planned a trip to South Texas. It was time to start looking for land and a homestead, while getting acquainted with the Valley bordering the Rio Grande River.

***

CHAPTER 2—
Discovering South Texas

Once the papers were signed and Sylvia returned to the University, it was time to prepare to move. Nellie and Wilma started packing personal and household items into large railroad crates that would be brought to the railroad for shipment to Laredo. Their job was to literally empty the house and barn of all small items. This left the large furniture which would be picked up by the local freight company.

Stan started herding the cattle to bring them to the Dallas railroad stock yards. The final count before starting the drive to Dallas came to a total of 829 head of cattle of which 170 were yearlings (109 steers and 61 heifers). The market value of full-size animals was down to $17 per head and $10 for yearling steers, and $8 for yearling heifers. The drought had caused havoc with the animals and their market value. Stan had no choice but to accept the offered price before October 1st. The grand total came to just under $13,000. Stan paid off the drovers he had hired for the drive and then deposited $2,500 into five accounts as had been agreed.

Once the herd was sold, Stan and family found a nice home with a small barn in Dallas. They moved with all their personal belongings, two horses and one of the family buggies. Stan had a comfortable bank account and was about to start an apprentice job with Humble Oil on a well drilling rig.

Meanwhile, Grant and Brian had packed two large traveling cases, two scabbards, one rifle, one shotgun along with their Colt revolvers and other miscellaneous items when traveling on horseback. The one item that was not routine was the fact that they were each carrying $1000 in cash in their money belt. It was Brian who asked, "dad, why are we carrying so much cash?"

"Because, we are going to the Valley to buy land and hopefully a homestead. If we find both, we'll try to buy horses, tack, wagons, implements and whatever large items we can get in the town on the westside of the Valley—the town that developed around the Santa Anna Ranch owned by the McAllen family. Also, that is why we are well armed, to deter any criminal interest in our presence."

Once ready they took the train to Laredo Texas. The first leg left Dallas at 7AM and covered the 275 miles to San Antonio in eight hours. There, they had an overnight stay in San Antonio before they took the train to Laredo the next morning.

Arriving in San Antonio, Grant said, "it's tiring to sit for eight hours with very little activity. Yet it's better to cover 275 miles in eight hours than to travel eight days on horseback to cover the same distance. Anyways, let's get a room at the railroad hotel, drop our long guns, travel cases and saddlebags, and then get dinner in one of the diners."

The next morning, the Cassidys were at the railroad platform at 5AM. The train was on time and by 6AM they were rolling towards Laredo. During the trip, the conductor announced that once in Laredo, the railroad had an arrangement with the steamboat Captains. A steamboat would be waiting at the dock for passengers who are traveling to the Valley. Plus, a wagon would pick them up at the yard to transfer them to the waiting steamer. The boat fare would be paid on embarking.

After the conductor's announcement, Grant

went to the privy. Brian knew that he had now placed some small bills in one pant pocket and some large bills in the other pocket--the rule was that you never pull out your money belt in public and never show any cash more than is needed.

Another passenger had noticed Grant's activity as well. He introduced himself as Gary Sweeney, Vice President of the Merchant's Bank in the Valley. "Your maneuver was wise, but I'm not the only one who noticed what you did. I presume you gentlemen are coming to the Valley to buy real-estate and you have cash in your money belt."

"Yes. We did not know if there was a bank in the Valley, or whether anyone would accept bank vouchers from Dallas."

"Well you can start bank accounts in our bank, and I guarantee you that everyone within a hundred miles will accept your bank vouchers drawn on our bank."

"Very good, we will do that."

"Now what is your goal in buying land in the valley?"

"We want to start a commercial vegetable growing enterprise."

"Well let me explain some very important issues. There are two towns of 500 people in the

Valley and they are both at the ends of the 30 mile Valley. The one on the east will likely get the railroad from Houston in five years. Beyond the 30-mile Valley, your product would have to travel by river back to Laredo or east downriver to Brownsville." For a local market, depend on my town of 500 people to the west and the other settlements to the east—for a span of ten miles. In that ten-mile span, there are several communities that drain into my town and would provide you with a large local market. In five years when the railroad comes west from Brownsville, you'll be ready to expand and start shipping your product by train. Plus, there is another advantage. You can order materials from Laredo and have a choice of cheaper land freighting or water transport by steamer for quicker deliveries."

Mr. Sweeney landed the final benefit, "I travel to San Antonio once a week to transfer money, documents and get whatever signatures are needed to finalize business transactions at the parent bank. I even pick up emergency packages and send telegrams for our customers and merchants. We try to service our clients and our town's people."

"Plus, let's not forget our town provides the

following services: Two doctors, one dentist, a dry goods food store and general merchandise, a hardware store, a feed and grain store, two diners, a gun/leather shop, a dressmaker, a saddler, a hotel, three saloons, two lawyers, a courthouse, a town clerk/property tax/land office, a real-estate office in my bank and a sheriff's office with a sheriff. The town square is the location for the local farmer's market."

"Well Mr. Sweeney, you've convinced me. We'll be in your bank to start an account and make a large deposit. Then we will talk to your real-estate agent."

"And that would be me, please call me Gary. What are you after for your business venture?"

"Ok, we are Grant and Brian Cassidy, please call me Grant. We are looking for riverside land with a central homestead within five miles of your town."

Gary appeared shocked and said, "this is serendipity, the bank owns a nice homestead that they inherited. An elderly and sickly couple lived on a small five-acre homestead with their only source of income was selling chicken eggs. They had not paid their mortgage or property taxes for two years. Upon their deaths, the bank inherited the homestead and had to pay the back taxes. The place has been for sale for two years at a price that would allow the bank to make up their loss at a small profit. The problem is that it's too expensive for local people to buy. I'm certain that the bank president would offer it at a decent price."

"That is interesting, but is there any land for sale adjacent to this homestead?"

"Yes, the tax collector and the railroad land agent have recently told me that there is plenty of land for sale, to the east and west of the homestead, at 25-40 cents per acre."

"Do you know what the bank is asking for the homestead?"

"Yes, the current list price is $700. It consists of a four-bedroom two-story house, a large barn that holds ten horses, a chicken coop that held 150 chickens, a carriage house with several wagons and a windmill well that is still active. Plus, the house is completely furnished."

"That appears to be a lot of reasonably priced real-estate. As soon as we can rent horses, we'll be over to check it out"

"And I'll be glad to show it to you."

The five-hour trip to Laredo came to an end and the transfer to the steamship was quickly and smoothly accomplished. As they boarded the ship, it became clear that it was a double decker ferry. Half of the lower deck was the livestock section; the other half was for freight and the privy. The people were held on the top deck with some light meals and liquid refreshments.

It was another five-hour trip which landed them in the Valley's western town. Grant and Brian took a room in the Winslow Hotel and had dinner at one of the local diners—Kate's Diner. After a good night's sleep, they were back in Kate's Diner for a hearty breakfast of steak and eggs and coffee. After breakfast, they went to the Merchant's Bank and opened an account and deposited $1,800 in cash and a $1,000 voucher from their Dallas bank. Afterwards they went to Craven's Livery where they met Sammy Craven.

"Hello, we are Grant and Brian Cassidy and we would like to rent a couple of saddled horses."

"How about these two chestnut geldings?"

"They're fine, how much?"

"50 cents a day for each."

Grant and Brian then made their way to the land office with the assistance of Gary Sweeney. The railroad agent greeted them, and Gary asked to see the map of available land surrounding the

McDonald property. It was clear that for a mile to the east and west of the homestead, the land was all for sale at a cost of 40 cents per acre for river frontage and 25 cents per acre for inland lots. After picking up some water for their canteens, they went to Stevenson's Mercantile for a can of beans, a pound of bacon, a pound of coffee, a loaf of homemade bread—their lunch while on the trail.

Heading east, Grant was reading the land. The river banks were high to minimize spring flooding. The land had a slow downhill course great for irrigation. The soil was a sandy dark loam similar to central Texas. There were few trees to hamper cultivation. There were no rocks. The land was flat. It had many positive features and no drawbacks.

Arriving at the first buildings, Gary said, "this is the McDonald homestead. The yards showed lack of attention for the past years. The building looked great from the outside. Tying their horses to the railing, they stepped on a full covered porch. The entrance parlor had a heating stove and nice sitting furniture. The kitchen had a gorgeous main table with eight chairs. The pantry was a walk-in type with a stairway that went into a cold cellar. The sink had its own water source from the windmill well and the fancy cookstove looked like new. Cabinets were full of pots, pans, dishes, plates, cups and silverware. The backdoor to the privy had its own porch. The only other rooms on the first floor was the master bedroom with ample closet and bureaus, and a small office. The office had a gun rack, safe, storage, file cabinets and desk. The upstairs had three bedrooms that were all fully furnished.

After the house came the barn. This was a sturdy structure with stalls for 10 horses and room for several extra ones. The second floor had a pulley to lift hay bales to the loft. A hand pump well provided water for the horses. Attached to the barn was a lean-to that had a large wagon, a buckboard and a personal buggy—all in good condition.

The chicken coop was a surprise. It was well built and even insulated for winter months. It was surrounded by a sturdy hardware fence of web fencing that would prevent predators from entering. It was so large that it certainly could hold a commercial production of chickens and eggs.

The last part of the inspection was looking at

the five acres. It was completely open and mostly showed signs of past cultivation. It was clear that the last years of the McDonalds life was spent living off the sale of their horses, chickens and cultivating implements.

After the building inspection, they traveled to the east of the homestead to find the same land layout as it was to the west of the homestead. Returning to the homestead, Grant entered the house with all the food he had brought for lunch. They started a fire in the cookstove, added their canteen water to make coffee, cooked the pound of bacon and added the beans at the end. That, plus homemade bread to dip in the bacon grease, provided a great lunch.

As Brian was busy cooking the bacon, Grant said, "we would be happy to buy this homestead at your stated price. On our way back to town we will stop to buy the adjoining lands. Do you agree son?

"Oh yeah, heck I already feel like I'm home!"

After a great lunch, the party went back to town. Grant and Brian went straight to the land office. "We have checked out the area and would like to buy some land."

"Good, the railroad is eager to sell some land

to finance their building of more tracks. How much land do you want and where?"

"We would like one mile of river frontage to the west of the McDonald homestead and one mile north inland to make it a full section of 640 acres. Plus, the same amount to the east of the McDonald homestead. For a total of two sections or 1280 acres."

"Half of this acreage is river frontage that sells for 40 cents per acre and the inland acreage sells for 25 cents per acre. Now the railroad reserves the right to build a railroad through your land at no cost to them. But whenever crossing agricultural land, they build a track crossing every half to three quarter miles, so you can cross your wagons without difficulty. In your case, you would end up with three crossings and I will enter this exception in your bill of sale."

After calculations are done the manager says, "that will be $416."

Grant pulls out a local bank draft and pays for the land. Before they leave, they were given a deed in the names of Grant, Nellie, Sylvia and Brian Cassidy.

Their next stop was the bank. They paid the $700 and were given a deed in the same four names. Their final stop was the tax collector. Grant showed them the two deeds which the tax collector duly registered. Then Grant paid the taxes on the homestead and land for the next two years. That total came to $114.

Later that evening, Grant and Brian were having a wonderful dinner at Josephine's Diner. They were enjoying a steak dinner with mashed potatoes and fresh corn. During the meal, Brian said, "we were lucky to find a homestead only five miles from town and surrounded with all that land for under $1300—with paid taxes for two years. Now I've been thinking about this and I think I should stay here and start cultivating the land around the homestead. We will need to buy some work horses and implements to include a two-way plow, disc and finish harrows. I will need to buy a horse for traveling to town, some more clothes and food. I will want your rifle along with my shotgun for handling predators. I will even start ordering chickens to get the coop occupied. There is so much I can do to start getting things started. What do you say?"

"I think it's a great idea, but what will your mother say and what will she do to me, coming home without you?"

"Just remind her that I'm 22 years old and can take care of myself. Just keep telling her the great news about this homestead and she'll get over it."

***

The next morning after a good night's sleep and a full breakfast at Kate's Diner, Grant and Brian went shopping. If Brian was to stay in the Valley, he needed cultivating implements within a reasonable time frame. So, their first stop was Emerson's Hardware. As they walked in, Brian took the lead.

"Good morning, are you Mr. Emerson?"

"Yes, and you are?"

After introductions and their reason for moving to the Valley, Brian said, "we're in need of cultivating implements. Can you help us out?"

"Normally, I order such large items from the plant in San Antonio. It usually takes a week to ten days to get them here, but you are in luck today. A few weeks ago, the salesman sent over three of the new models. I was going to keep them as a display but decided to sell them and not carry such expensive items. Let me show them to you."

The new implements had some minor improvements but basically were the same implements they had in Dallas. Brian said, "how much for all three?"

"$425 for all three, delivered at the McDonald house."

"We'll take them."

"Great, what kind of payment schedule would you like?"

"I'll pay with a bank voucher off your Merchant's Bank and would like to start a family credit account for goods. I will give you a deposit of $50 to open the account since I know I'll be back for supplies."

The deal was done, and Mr. Emerson said, "please call me Floyd and thank you for your business. Welcome to the Valley and good luck."

The next stop was the Craven Livery. Sammy greeted them and asked what they needed?

Brian answered, "well, I just bought a plow and harrows, so I need some work horses."

"Come with me to the back corral, I have a pair of Percherons."

The pair was a matched white/silver set. They appeared young and healthy. Sammy added, "This team comes with nearly new harnesses and it's an experienced team working cultivation equipment. Plus, they are both smart and gentle."

"How much for the pair plus that saddled gelding I'm renting from you?"

"All three shod with new shoes comes to $240."

"Seems a bit high, what do you think dad?"

"I agree, but without work horses and transportation to town you are dead in the water."

Sammy realized that these men could be a long-term investment for his livery, so he said, "as new business customers, I'll knock off $30 for $210 with new shoes, saddle and two harnesses. Plus, my helper will deliver the Percherons to your homestead."

Brian shook Sammy's hand and paid him with a bank voucher.

Grant pointed out to Brian that he needed to establish credit accounts at other businesses. So, they visited Stevenson's Mercantile, Caldwell's Feed and Seed, and McClintock's Freighting. At each location they introduced themselves and their business venture. Accounts with the four family names were started and a $50 deposit left in each account.

At the feed store, Brian paid and arranged

for a delivery of hay, straw, 24 chickens, chicken mash, oyster shells, and bags of oats.

Freighting to their homestead from the steamboat cargoes were a straight forward fee for delivery, to McClintock and the boat Captain. Orders coming by land would be delivered by the same company which held their main office in Laredo, and a satellite office in town—one fee.

After buying several sets of clothes and other personal items, Brian chose the dry goods, fresh meat, eggs and produce to fill his pantry and cold cellar.

With Brian properly organized to start work on the land, Grant packed his travel case and took the boat back to Laredo where he transferred to the train back to Dallas. Grant had plenty of time on the train to plan the family move to the Valley. The biggest issue was which large items were cheaper to ship versus ordering once in the Valley.

***

CHAPTER 3—Settling in the Valley

When Grant arrived at the Dallas station, he was greeted by Nellie and Sylvia. They were both shocked to find Brian missing. After Grant assured both that Brian was fine, the two ladies were full of questions. Grant interrupted them and said, "yes we have a new homestead to include a beautiful house, large barn and plenty of land. Now I'm starved, so let's go to the house and I'll tell you all about it."

While traveling, Grant asked what the two had been doing during his trip. Nellie said, "we have packed every small item from the house and barn that would fit in the crates provided by the railroad. We have filled three crates and the bare essentials in clothing and kitchen cooking utensils are left for the fourth and final crate. The only things left are the large items such as implements, horses, wagons and windmills."

Arriving home, Nellie started cooking dinner and Sylvia made the coffee and set the table. Grant started talking, and the ladies listened attentively without interrupting him. After a long hour of talking, eating dinner and cleaning the dishes, Nellie and Sylvia started with questions Nellie started, "if the new house has better furniture than what is here, what are we going to do with all this furniture?"

"Call the auction house, have them pick this all up, sell it, take their fees and give us the balance."

"Ok, what did you mean the cook stove is a new model with accessories?"

"The stove has a cooking oven next to the firebox on one side and a hot water tank on the other side of the firebox. This allows you to always have heated water available for use. Plus, it has a warming oven on top of the stove. When the stove is not used for cooking, it has a vented panel that you can open to help heat the kitchen if needed."

"Very good, we may have packed a duplicate in the eating utensils, but with two children of marrying age, I'm sure we'll find a home for these things, heh?"

Sylvia then took over the questioning and discussion. We have six windmills that can be dismantled and packed in crates. If we bring the modifications to turn a well windmill into a transfer pump, we'll have the beginning of an irrigation system. Is it worth the extra savings to ship or order once in the Valley?"

"When I had a layover in San Antonio, I met with the yard manager. We compared shipping horses, implements, wagons and such things as dismantled windmills in crates. In every instance, the shipping was only 20% of the replacement value, and the items would arrive within a week's time—even arrive before we get there. So, ship anything you think we will need."

Sylvia looked at her dad and said, "this is what I will ship:"

1. "A shade house frame with a shatter proof glass roof, screen shades for the ceiling and walls, tarps to enclose the house in the winter and a ducted coal stove to keep safe temperatures in the winter."
2. "Greenhouse tubes, pots, potting soil ingredients and tools."
3. "New implements, a potato planter and harvester, a line seeder or grain mill, a hand pushed seeder, a manure spreader, an irrigation ditch adapter for the plow, a

> pH soil tester and a horse drawn transplant planter."

The next day, Grant and Sylvia went to make arrangements with the railroad manager for: four standard crates, six windmill crates with pump modifications, a plow, a disc harrow, a finish harrow, all the extensive items on Sylvia's list, a medium size utility wagon, Grant's vegetable display wagon and five horses—two Belgium work horses, one riding horse with saddle and two large geldings for wagon and light duty implements with saddles for occasional riding.

The total cost was $1,000 which included freighting from Laredo to the Valley by slow wagon, and it also included tickets for four passengers to Laredo and then passage by steamboat to the Valley. Using this method, the Cassidys would arrive before the freight did.

The only chore left to do was the dismantling. Grant and Sylvia would dismantle the windmill once it was lowered to the ground by horsepower. After crating the parts with the pump adapter, Nellie would drive the wagon and deliver the windmill crate to the railroad yard. During this time, the freighting company brought the implements and loaded them onto a box car that was storing the other items and crates. The last day, they packed the fourth crate with food, kitchen items and personal items and were ready to move.

The entire family stayed in the railroad hotel until their five horses finally arrived. With their own box car loaded, they started their journey to a new land—but still in Texas.

***

Meanwhile, Brian had gotten accustomed to his routine of plowing every morning and running the disc harrows in the afternoons after a long lunch break for his Percherons. One day, as he was putting his horses in the barn, he heard a wagon approach. Coming outside he saw a buckboard full of supplies and the seat holding an older man with a younger woman at his side. The gentlemen said, "we are your neighbors two miles to the east and we are adjoining your new land. I'm Elmer Adams and this is my daughter Jenna. My wife Beth is holding the homestead. Elmer continued talking in generalities, but Brian only heard the name of the young lady. She was slim, tall with short black hair, and had nice female attributes. He realized he was staring at her, but she was doing the same. Suddenly, he heard the gentlemen say, "well, it's been nice meeting you and come over some time to see my commercial hay operation."

As the Adams left, Brian had to shake himself into reality. During his dinner, he thought of several reasons and ways to find himself visiting the Adams homestead. The next day, he went back to plowing. At noon, as he was watering the horses, a horse was entering the yard. Brian looked up and saw Jenna on horseback carrying a bag. Brian says, "welcome neighbor, step down and sit a spell."

"Mom and I baked some bread and I thought it would be neighborly to welcome you properly. These are whole white breads."

"Wow, they are still warm. Why don't you join me for lunch? I have some butter and homemade jelly. With a cup of coffee, we can enjoy your bread and visit."

"Sure, that would be nice!"

Two hours later, they were still talking. Brian shared his years in Dallas and his recent interest in establishing a commercial vegetable enterprise.

Jenna admitted that she enjoyed life as it was on the Rio Grande. She liked housekeeping, cooking, gardening and helping her dad in the horse barn as well as helping with hay harvesting and storage. Her job was adding string to the hay as it was being baled in the new one-horse baler.

Eventually, Jenna realized that it was nearly 3PM and said, "Oh my goodness, we've been talking for hours and you need to get back to work, heh!"

"Talking to you is very easy, I could continue till dinner time and not run out of subject matter."

"Maybe I can come back another day, Ok?"

"Anytime."

Several days went by and Brian hoped to see Jenna arrive at lunch time, but it never happened. A few days later, as he was leading his work horses into the barn, there stood Jenna with her britches covered in hay chaff. The barn had been cleaned, picked up and the spare harness had been oiled with leather grease. Bales of hay were stacked on the main floor. Brian simply said, "what on earth are you up to?"

"Well, I was bored at home and I guess it showed. My mom saw thru me and suggested I come here to help out."

Brian simply stepped up to her and did something totally out of his character. He took Jenna into his arms and kissed her. The kiss was prolonged and finally Jenna said, "wow, that is pretty good pay for my afternoon's work. By the way, my dad is offering you a pair of work horses to help you cultivate until your family arrives with more equipment and horses. Along with the horses, I am included as free labor if it's Ok with you!"

And that is how it all started. That night after a long passionate kiss, they each slept in different bedrooms. The next morning, Jenna helped Brian harness the work horses. Jenna hitched her team to the disc harrows and Brian continued plowing. During a long rest period at lunch, Elmer showed up to see how everything was going. It was after Jenna whispered in her dad's ear that Elmer left with a smile on his face.

With Elmer gone, Brian asked Jenna what she had told her dad. "That's privileged information that ……….as Brian kissed her and his hands started roaming. Jenna started groaning with pleasure. "Now, are you going to tell me, or do I torture you some more?"

"Keep torturing me!"

"Goodness, woman. What am I going to do with you? I have never been in love, but I am now. Would you marry me?"

"I've also fallen in love with you, and of course I'll marry you."

After more affectionate kissing, Jenna said, "I told dad that I was still chaste but that I was going to marry you."

So, during the next weeks, they worked and slept together as a committed couple. A wedding would be planned after the arrival of the Cassidy family from Dallas and Jenna's brother, Max, from San Antonio.

***

A week later, Brian received a telegram from Dallas. They would be in Laredo by September 30th and would be at the Valley dock with their five horses the next day via a river ferry.

Brian and Jenna were waiting at the dock. When they disembarked Brian was covered in hugs and kisses. All of a sudden, Nellie spotted Jenna and asked, "pray tell, who is this lovely lady waiting in the sideline?"

"Mom, dad and Sylvia, meet the girl of my

dreams, my soul-mate, my best friend and my loving fiancé. This is Jenna Adams, soon to be Mrs. Brian Cassidy." Hugs, kisses and congratulations started all over again—this time to include Jenna.

On the way home, Nellie and Sylvia were sitting on the buckboard seat with Jenna. The family travel bags were in the back. Brian and Grant were riding their horses and trailing the two Belgiums and the two work geldings. As soon as they got home from the four-mile trip, they all sat around the kitchen table and Brian told his story. He said, "I started cultivating the land, but it was a slow process alone. Then I met Jenna who turned out to be our neighbor. Jenna's dad lent us two work horses which allowed me to do the plowing and Jenna did all the harrowing. We now have 80 acres ready for planting and irrigation."

Sylvia added, "and when did you have time for romance?"

Jenna answered, "during water breaks, lunch, dinner and bedtime. It's pretty easy when your relationship not only feels right, but you know that it is right. We are so much in love that we don't even believe it ourselves. As soon as you meet my parents and my single brother arrives from San Antonio, we will be wed by Pastor Wilbrook at St. Eugene church in town. Arrangements need to be made for a meal in the parish hall, catered by Kate's Diner."

Grant asks, "what does your dad and brother do for a livelihood?"

"My dad is a commercial hay and oats grower and supplies the Valley with local hay, straw and oats. My brother is a Bounty Hunter and a sort of protector for valley inhabitants."

Sylvia countered, "With a sheriff in town and Texas Rangers as border security, why do we need Bounty Hunters?"

"Border security is a very complicated issue, and I would prefer to let Max explain it to you."

Nellie added, "so when do we meet your parents and brother?

"My mom and dad will be over tonight—they only live a mile away next to your land. They have also invited our neighbors and friends to a social evening for you to meet everyone. That event will occur once my brother arrives.

That evening the Cassidys met the Adams. Grant and Nellie immediately struck it with Elmer and Bessie. The men could see a symbiotic relationship where they could share some of their horses and implements as well as barter back and forth for animal feed and vegetables. Bessie and Nellie saw a friendship developing where they could share their work and hobbies.

The next day crates started arriving. Grant had arranged to send two crates of personal items, three crates of windmills, and two crates of shade house parts to be sent by water cargo. The remainder of the crates, implements, and wagons would arrive by slower land freighting which would take at least four more days.

Grant and Brian started work on the first windmill. They built four concrete leg footings and spent two days reassembling the windmill and installing the modification that converted the well to a water pump transfer. The six windmills would be erected along the mile west of the homestead. That meant the windmills would be approximately 900 feet apart. Grant saw early in the installation that a holding pond would have to be built for each windmill in preparation of the needed irrigation. It was Elmer who suggested contacting a neighboring Mexican group of workers to dig the ponds. To Grant's surprise, the going wage for Mexican workers was 50 cents a day in US funds. Grant hired ten workers who managed to dig a half acre four-foot-deep pond in seven days.

Meanwhile, Nellie was busy unpacking the two crates of personal items—mostly clothing and kitchen items. Sylvia and Jenna started putting up the framing for the shade/glass house by using stock items in the crate and local 2X4 lumber. When a wall was ready for lifting, the men came to help.

After several days of shade/glass house construction, Sylvia and Jenna managed to share their past lives. Jenna realized that Sylvia was a bright and pleasant person, and simply a pleasure to be with. She silently thought how lucky she was to have such a wonderful person for a sister-in-law.

After a week passed, the men had all three windmills upright, and the girls had their shade/glass house nearly finished. They were waiting for the coal ducted stove to arrive as well as a load of coal.

Next, everyone got together and using local lumber, they enlarged the wagon shed to hold more implements known to be on their way.

Finally, Jenna's brother arrived, and the Adams held a "welcome to the neighborhood party" with all the homesteaders living along the ten mile stretch of Valley leading back to the town. It promised to be a gala event with a keg of beer, a pig roast and a country dance.

Shortly after arrival, Sylvia went to thank the Adams for hosting such a wonderful evening. She went up to Elmer who had his back to her. She tapped him on the shoulder, and as he turned, the earth stopped turning. Sylvia froze, as she saw a young man with Jenna's looks, a million-dollar smile on his face and wearing his Colt as well as the Sheriff's badge on his vest.

The young man doffed his hat and said, "Miss Sylvia Cassidy, I presume!"

Sylvia's brain stopped functioning momentarily, but as she recovered, she extended her hand and said, "nice to finally meet you, I presume you're Max, and no less the sheriff, heh!"

***

BOOK TWO

MAX

CHAPTER 4—The Beginning

Max Adams had a golden childhood. Being raised with his younger sister, Jenna, he enjoyed her as a playmate and nearly an equal since they were only eleven months apart. When school started, he and Jenna would travel the five miles to school every day. Mom and dad made the sacrifice of driving them each day since they both believed that an education was necessary in the pre-1900 era.

By the time Max was ten, the two would ride double on an old mare and would stable her in Sammy's livery during school. Dad would gladly pay the stabling fees and save two trips to town each day. Max enjoyed school. He liked to learn and make friends with the kids in school. Although he liked being home, school was a great escape. Whereas Jenna liked being home and working with horses in the field.

Speaking of money, the Adams never were short of food and the living essentials. Early on, Elmer had seen the need for horse feed, especially for those living in town and other small settlements. After buying one of the early hay balers, he invested in cultivating, and harvesting equipment. Although he never expanded beyond his half section of 320 acres, he was able to support his family and provide a reasonable product for his local customers.

By the age of twelve, Max was Elmer's helper. He was taking care of the barn and horses, caring for the chickens, and helping with the irrigation. Yet by age fourteen, Max was experiencing a drive towards his real love, firearms. Since Elmer only used a shotgun to shoot predators, he realized Max needed guidance that he could not provide. Seeking help from an old friend, Omer McClellan, Max went to work in his gun shop every day after school and all-day Saturday.

As arranged with Elmer, Omer handed Max a brand-new Colt 45 pistol/speed holster. His pay would be 50 cents a week to be applied towards payment of the $25 Colt. In addition, Max could have all the ammo he reloaded during his time at home—one round for him and one round for Omer to sell. Omer was happy with this arrangement since he enjoyed working with

Max, and that way he would stay on the job for a guaranteed year.

During that year, Omer taught Max how to properly do a fast draw, point and shoot with one hand and how to be accurate to 50 yards with two hand shooting. Once the basics were well engrained, Max would practice before school, after work, before dark, and Sunday after church. A combination of several short practices each day plus one long day provided the experience to become a shootist—which he had become by the age of fifteen.

Max was a quick learner and by the age of fifteen was not just cleaning and performing action jobs on pistols and rifles but started doing repairs. Omer commented to Elmer that Max could understand the relationship of each moving part and its relationship to other parts. It was like Max had an extra dimension in his brain.

For his fifteenth birthday, Elmer and Omer got together and gave Max a Winchester 1876 rifle with an 8X Malcolm scope. It also included a bullet mold and reloader for the 1876 cartridge. Again, Omer showed him how to do freestyle rifle shooting and how to make adjustments for windage and elevation using the dials on the Malcolm scope.

Omer would miss Max during the months of June—August when Max would help his dad with the important hay and oats harvests. By September 1st, the work was backing up. Yet not one of the customers would complain since they all knew that Max's magic hands would return by September. When Max finished school at the age of sixteen, Omer hired him full time, except June—August, and paid him $1 a day plus the free ammo at the same 50-50 ratio.

That last year at home is when Jenna announced she wanted to be proficient with a rifle and pistol. Max agreed to teach her, but under the condition that Jenna had to reload her own ammunition. The other thing that happened before reaching the age of eighteen is that Elmer saw the writing on the wall. Max would be leaving home on his eighteenth birthday. In preparation, Elmer hired a nearby Mexican worker as a seasonal employee on the homestead to cover spring to late fall.

A week after his eighteenth birthday, and event occurred in town. The Merchants Bank was robbed, and a cashier was killed. The robbers were made up of a notorious six-member gang of mixed

Mexicans and Americans under the leadership of Butcher Kellogg. Sheriff McFarlane and a small posse gave chase to the Rio Grande, but once across the river into Mexico, the American lawmen had to abandon their chase. It was always difficult for the locals in town to accept this international agreement. Only private bounty hunters could go across the border to Mexico and bring back criminals—dead or alive.

Upon the posse's return, there was a gathering of townsfolks outside the bank. One man asks, "how much was stolen and what is the reward for getting your money back?"

The bank president said, "$3,000 and the reward is $300 plus all the private bounties offered for their capture—dead or alive."

Max was eyeing the man asking these questions. "Sir, are you planning to go after this bunch of dirt bags by yourself?"

"Yes son, why do you ask?"

"Because I want to learn to be a Bounty Hunter. I'm very good with a pistol and all firearms, I'm a quick learner, I'll be loyal to you and I'll cover your back. I'm ready to take a bullet to save your life. You have nothing to lose except half the rewards."

The bounty hunter looked at the young man and could see something special in his eyes and demeanor. He instinctively said, "70-30 and get your guns, gear and horse. My name is Wes Silvers. We're leaving in an hour."

"Yes sir, my name is Max Adams and I'll be back before the hour."

***

Wes was a determined rider and pushed his horse to the animal's ability and tolerance. Max could follow but didn't have the time to do any tracking. Fortunately, Wes lead the way and did the tracking. Being two hours behind the outlaws, it was assumed that they would not catch up to Butcher Kellogg and his band of murderers today. When darkness arrived, Wes stopped at a grassy area with running water and a backstop of a rocky ledge. After unsaddling and theddering each horse on a long rope so they could crop hay and drink without mixing their ropes, Wes set up camp.

Max said, "I'm not accustomed to setting up a trail camp, so how can I help you."

"Gather some wood and watch me, so you can set up camp next time."

Wes dug a firepit and started a cooking fire that would not show a significant flame and would be extinguished after the meal was cooked. He then brought his extra saddlebags. On one side he took out a coffee pot, cooking pan, coffee tins, forks and spoons. On the other side he took out a can of beans, a slab of bacon, Arbuckle's Ariosa coffee, and some hardtack. Wes added, "this is your basic food stuff for breakfast and dinner. For lunch its usually beef jerky in the saddle. When you stop in a town, get what extra you can at a dry goods mercantile. It is always nice to add eggs, crackers, cheese, a ham, bread, biscuits, potatoes, onions, canned beef, flour—with the last four you can make a beef stew."

After dinner, Wes took the cooking and eating utensils to the stream for cleaning.

Max had been observing very carefully. He then asked, "why do you have four bedrolls tied behind your saddle.?"

"Only one is a double layered bedroll. The other three are for rainy days and nights: a tent, a tarp and a rain slicker. When you're on the trail of outlaws, rain can't stop you, but you must remain dry to stay on their trail."

Getting ready for bedding down, Wes laid out his bedroll some ten yards away from camp and behind a boulder. He then took his tarp, laid it flat and filled it with grass and twigs, rolled it up and put it next to where the camp fire had been. Max asked, "why are you doing this?"

"Because, if we get visitors during the night that our horses did not detect, and the visitors start shooting, they'll be shooting holes in my tarp, not me. Remember, just because we are the ones chasing outlaws doesn't mean that they can't decide to eliminate us with lead poisoning."

"I presume that's why you brought the horses close to camp and ground hitched them."

"Correct. When the danger is high of visitors, I tie a fine durable black rope six inches off the ground and tied between trees. A visitor who trips on the rope will usually accidentally discharge his firearm."

Upon retiring to their bedrolls, Wes laid his sawed-off shotgun next to the right side of his bedroll, and his pistol to his left. Max did the same with his pistol.

The night was uneventful and after a breakfast

of bacon, hardtack soaked with bacon grease and coffee, they were back on the trail. Stopping in two hours to rest and water the horses, Max asked, "do you think we'll catch up with them today"

"No, unless I'm mistaken, we are approaching a small Mexican settlement and if we are lucky, we might find out where they were headed."

While the horses rested and did some foraging, Wes took the opportunity to explain something important. "As a bounty hunter in a foreign land, there are two types of Mexicans you'll be dealing with. Of course, there are the locals called Nationals and these cannot be touched (legally) unless they are committing a crime in the US. That is the responsibility of the local sheriff and the Texas Rangers. The other group of Mexicans you will be dealing with are those who moved to the US years ago to either become workers or homesteaders. Some of these abandoned their families and took the easy way to survive, they became outlaws. These are the Mexicans we are dealing with now and in the future. Just because they have a Mexican heritage, they are your enemy and you must treat them just like the American outlaws—either in the US or Mexico. Now this

Kellogg band has two Mexicans, any question about their loyalty and murderous intent?"

"No sir, I'm following your drift and you can rely on me."

Shortly after getting back on the trail, they arrived at a small town. Being early morning, the cantina was not open, so Wes rode directly to the local store called the "Mercantil." As they entered, they both met an elderly gentleman who had a black eye. He spoke passable English and when asked what had happened to get the shiner, he said, "a band of Americans and Mexicans picked up supplies and tried to leave without paying. When I called the leader on it, he punched me in the face, and I was knocked down. They left laughing and I didn't do anything since I was so glad that they left without destroying my merchandise or the front windows."

"What did the leader look like?"

"Huge man, weighing over 300 pounds, long greasy black hair and a full beard. He smelled bad as did most of his band of miscreants."

"That man was Butcher Kellogg. What is the value of their pillaging?

"With the ten bottles of whiskey it came up to $16.87 in US."

"Any idea which direction they took? Did they go to the local Cantina or head out of town?"

"I heard the leader say they were going to 'Grande,' some twenty miles to the west. With all the whiskey they had, I don't think they got far before setting up camp and getting drunk. That likely means they are still sleeping off the night's binge. If you are after them, I suspect they are still in camp. Be careful, these are dangerous men who have nothing to lose."

"Thank you for your help, here is a double eagle for your goods and your help."

"Senor, this is $25 in US. I cannot accept it."

"Not negotiable. Adios and we will stop here for supplies after we catch this bunch—or whatever is left of them."

Within a half hour, they came up to a grassy field and their horses were seen from over a hundred yards. They ground hitched their horses and set out on foot to find their camp. Wes took his boots off and put on a pair of moccasins.

"What are moccasins for?"

"To sneak up on their camp without so much noise. Take your boots off and double layer your socks. Next time you'll have the proper footwear."

As they were about to start walking, Wes asked, "don't you have a shotgun instead of a scoped high-power rifle. This is going to be short distance shooting."

"No, this is my only backup firearm, I'll change that next time."

At 100 yards, Max could find five of the outlaws laying around the smoking campfire. One was missing and he told Wes. Max thought, *the scoped rifle had some advantages, but a good set of binoculars would work just as well.*

"More than likely, one went to the bushes during the night and was so drunk that he fell asleep on the ground. Expect him to show up once the shooting starts."

At 25 yards, Wes was about to yell out an announcement when Max, who was spotting the background camp boulders, spotted a man stand up. Max kept his scope on the man and when he saw him place his finger on the trigger, Max squeezed off his own trigger without any hesitation. Wes just about collapsed at the unexpected gun blast next to him. The man in the boulders was pushed back against a boulder and bounced off it to fall some 25 feet to the ground.

With the rifle shot, all five outlaws were up with their pistols drawn. Wes did not hesitate, he fired both barrels of his sawed-off shotgun and four of the outlaws went down. Wes found himself surprised when one man was left standing, Butcher Kellogg. Wes knew he would get shot before he pulled his own pistol. Suddenly the shot rang out and Wes saw a bloom of blood, fingers and wood chips from Kellogg's shooting hand. Kellogg screamed out and held what was left of his shooting hand. Missing was the wooden grip, three fingers and half of his shooting hand.

After they stopped the bleeding and secured Kellogg, Wes said, "I literally knew I was caught off guard and was about to die. Yet, you saved my life twice. You picked out that guard that I would have missed and took care of Kellogg. Can you really draw that Colt that fast? Plus, that was a lucky shot to his hand, but next time aim for the center of the heart instead."

"Well, I had no choice but to kill that guard in the rocks, he had his finger on the trigger and one of us was about to take a bullet. I had a choice with Kellogg. That outlaw needed to suffer and meet justice from a public hanging.

His butchering days of murder and mayhem are now over. That hand shot was an easy one."

Afterwards, Wes went through the dead men's pockets and saddlebags. The $3,000 was in Kellogg's saddlebags. They collected the pistols, rifles and anything else of value to include a compass, two pocket watches, and a new 50X binocular. The pocket cash amounted to +-$100. Wes gave Max $40 and pocketed the rest.

Max looked confused, "you gave me too much. I was supposed to get $30!"

"Changed my mind, the new ratio is 60-40. As soon as your apprentice days are over, we'll go to 50-50."

"When we get to town, we'll sell these horses, scabbards, saddles, saddlebags, pistols, rifles and split the profits. Don't forget, we will be getting bounty rewards which could amount to thousands. Now let's get these bodies back to town and Kellogg to Sheriff McFarlane's jail."

When they got to town the next day, the bodies were already beginning to smell. Sheriff McFarlane made an id on four by finding a name inside their hat band, or in the back of their holster or by an old letter in their saddlebags. One could not be identified, and Kellogg would not give the sheriff his name. Wes stepped up and shook Kellogg's hand, the shot up one. Kellogg screamed and nearly collapsed. Wes added, "if you want the doc to tend to your hand, you better spill out his name."

Sheriff McFarlane said he would send a telegram to the agencies offering the rewards via Gary Sweeney on his next trip to Laredo. For the next ten days, they stayed in the Winslow Hotel. They sold the six horses with saddles, scabbards, and saddlebags for $400. The six Colt pistols and 1873 rifles for $250. This divided dividend came up to $260 for Max. Wes convinced him to keep no more that was necessary to buy a sawed-off shotgun, moccassins, personal items and $50 cash in his pockets. The remainder of the money went in the Merchants Bank under his own account. In the future, reward money from other areas could be sent by telegram to their account in town via Gary Sweeney.

Ten days later, Gary arrived from Laredo with six telegraph vouchers to cover the rewards. Kellogg, who had already been hung, had a reward of $1500. All his band each had a reward of $750 each. The total came to $5,250 plus the $300 bank reward for returning the bank money.

Now Wes spoke up on how to disperse some of the funds.

"This is how we'll divide funds now and in the future. $250 goes to Sheriff McFarlane and his deputies for housing Kellogg and good will with the local law. The bank reward goes directly to the dead cashier's elderly widow along with $700 of our rewards. And last, we give Mr. Stevenson at the mercantile $300 to help needy homesteaders who cannot pay their credit bills. So that leaves us $4,000 which is a lot more than we deserve. You get $1,600 and you put that in the bank."

"I agree, this is certainly more money than we deserve."

"Well Max, look at it this way. Bounty hunting is a very dangerous profession. You have to be young and highly trained to stay alive. You can only do this for a few years. This is my fourth year and if it wasn't for a partner like you, I would have quit by now or only hunted after minor criminals that have rewards of less than $100 but with minimal risks of being shot."

"Ok then, let's make hay when the sun is shining. Where do we go from here since there's no more outlaws to chase in this town?"

Three days later, with a sawed-off 12-gauge

shotgun in a backpack holster, the bounty hunting duo took the ferry to Laredo. Little did they know that they would quickly become a legendary team of shotgun wielding gunfighters.

***

CHAPTER 5—Bounty Hunting Years

The first thing they did when they arrived in Laredo was to visit with Sheriff Handy. "Laredo has a population of about 1000 people. It is a major railroad terminal and a shipping center on the Rio Grande. Our little city has its share of troublemakers, petty theft, wife beatings, drunks and the occasional murder. Fortunately, with my three deputies, we can handle these law breakers. What the problem is in a town this size is bank robberies and train robberies. The Texas Rangers do their best in apprehending these outlaws, but when they head south to Mexico, they get away. Since we are so far away from San Antonio, very few bounty hunters come south since there is plenty of work there."

"So, if you plan to stick around, there'll be plenty of dangerous work for you. Although you won't get any help from me, I'll be glad to house your criminals pending trial and help you get your bounty hunting rewards."

"Now that is my pat statement to all bounty

hunters. Let me tell you of a new problem in this border town. Human trafficking!"

"What on earth is that?" Max asked.

"Kidnapping of American girls and bringing them to Mexican brothels or to rich Mexican landlords that want their own concubine. These kidnappers, both Americans and Mexicans, are career criminals that quickly wisp their victims into Mexico to keep the law at the river. This is the kind of criminal activity that requires a quick response of saviors, before they rape and ravage their victims on route to the brothels. For the lucky girls going to a rich Mexican landowner, there are extra days of reprieve before the inevitable result."

Wes added, "These kidnappings sound like an errand of mercy for bounty hunters. Where's the financial reward or is there any? We are willing to do our share of free work but cannot be the only ones doing it."

"Oh no. First of all, these American outlaws generally have a bounty on their heads, and even the Mexicans may also have a reward offered by the Mexican government. More important, the parents and husbands of these kidnapped victims often place high rewards to get their loved ones back. They know that if they don't quickly post a reward that after 48 hours, its likely that the victims will never be found."

"Ok, and we'll gladly pay for holding our arrests in your jail. Now can we look at your wanted posters and try to get a lead on some of these wanted outlaws?"

After spending quite some time at posters, Wes began to think that they all had the same artist making very similar faces. The only thing different was their hat, length of hair and amount of facial hair, plus a general description of their dress and peculiarities. It was Max who picked up a pattern. "Waldo Greene's gang of murderers had robbed two banks in Dallas, Houston, and two more in San Antonio. Doesn't it look like he's working his way south to Laredo?"

Sheriff Handy was impressed, "I think you have a good point. Let me send a few telegrams to local sheriffs, to see if they have a mode of operation we can look out for. We should get an answer by morning."

The next morning at least six telegrams came in. Sheriff Handy made a list of repeated similarities in their mode of operation. He then went to the hotel where Wes and Max were staying. They gathered in the hotel restaurant for breakfast and Sheriff Handy went through the list as they listened. The sheriff starts: "This gang likely arrives in town days before the robbery to gather information regarding the local payroll days. They gather every night in the same saloon but stay at different hotels. They rob the banks before closing to minimize a posse following after dark."

"They often neutralize the local sheriff and his deputies by forcing them into their own cells at gunpoint or killing them outright. They quickly shoot a cashier or a customer to speed up the collection of the money. Waldo Green takes the president aside and gets him to open the vault. If he refuses, he shoots him in the foot which always gets an open vault. They are bold and arrogant to come back in a week to rob another bank in the same town before they leave heading south."

Max added, "Ok, with this in mind, I believe they are already here preparing their robbery escapades. Wes and I will visit the hotels in town and try to isolate the ones who have single men as customers that gather in their restaurant as if they know each other.

Laredo had two large banks and a small branch of the Merchants Bank from the Valley.

Wes and Max visited the hotels in close proximity to the two large banks, the National and the Cattleman's Assoc. As expected, the Grand Hotel had three single entries. With a $5 bill on the counter, the clerk admitted that these three men would gather either at breakfast or lunch daily. Since they were now having breakfast, they went inside and ordered coffee. They committed the faces to memory and moved on.

Another hotel, the Executive Hotel, had a similar pattern of three more single entries. Waiting in the lobby for lunch time, the boys saw Waldo himself come down the stairs and enter the lunch room. Ten minutes later two ill clad men joined Waldo for lunch. Before leaving, another $5 bill on the counter revealed that this trio spent each night at the "Rusty Bucket."

Meeting with Sheriff Handy, the decision had to be made whether to arrest the gang now or wait till they attempted a robbery. Sheriff Handy favored the former method in hopes of saving lives. So, Wes and Max planned to arrest them once they got to the Rusty Bucket. However, they never showed up and later Wes found they had checked out of the hotel and Max found their horses gone from the nearby livery.

After the evening's revolting development, Wes said, "Max and I will pose as customers in the Cattleman's Assoc. and let's get the First National to close their doors for the day because of painting.

The next day an hour before bank closing, a rider arrived at the sheriff's office. He stepped off the boardwalk and entered with his pistol drawn. A deputy was standing behind the door and popped him on the head with a fire poker. That took care of that outlaw.

In the bank, Wes was standing behind a closed cashier's bench with his sawed-off shotgun under a ledger. Max was holding a depositor's pouch and was last in line. Max saw the five horses arrive, one man stayed on his horse and held the four horses' reins. Waldo and three men entered the bank. Waldo yells out, "this is a robbery, put your hands up or get shot."

Wes lets go his ledger, picks up the shotgun and firs at the outlaws. Everyone heard a loud click or a dud shotgun round. It surprised Wes so much that he seemed to forgot he had another shot available, or was it the feeling that his shotgun was broken? What ever the reason, he went for his Colt but knew the outlaws already had theirs drawn and pointed at him.

Seeing the entire circumstance unfolding, Max yells out, "stop and put your guns away. You're all under arrest!"

In slow motion to Max's eyes, the outlaws turned to face him and were all ready and planning to shoot him when two shots rang out and all four outlaws crumbled to the floor. Instantly, the sheriff entered the bank to see a sea of black gun smoke. He walked over to the four dead men and said, "how can there be four bodies, with a hole between the eyes, when I only heard two pistol shots?"

Wes answers, "because Max shoots so fast that two shots sound like one."

"Boy, you better keep that quiet because every gunfighter will come to challenge Max for the publicity."

Days later the two surviving bank robbers were transferred back to San Antonio where they could be tried for murder and robbery. Had they stood trial in Laredo, it would have been for an attempted robbery charge. The sheriff sent telegrams to organization that were offering rewards. The rewards came to $3,250. The sale of six saddled horses and 12 firearms came to $700. Sheriff Handy and deputies were paid $500 for capturing one outlaw and housing two in their jail. The usual $300 was given to a dry goods merchant to help pay for food to the needy. The balance of the money was divided between Wes and Max.

Weeks passed, and Laredo became a quiet community. Wes and Max decided to move north to San Antonio where the larger community had a higher major crime rate. The day of departure by train changed their lives forever. At the train depot, the talk was that a kidnapping ring had captured three well known young wives from local ranches, one was a large cattle baron's young wife. The talk was that it was a well-known crime syndicate from San Antonio that had sent a team of violent kidnappers to get a foothold in the community. The private rewards reached $10,000 in a matter of hours. When Max asked if anyone knew the direction these kidnappers took, everyone looked surprised. One man said, "well of course, north to the brothels of Houston and beyond. They'll be traveling by horses since they can't take the train with hostages."

Wes asked when this happened, "apparently

during the night. The husbands were overwhelmed, tied and gagged and the wives gagged to keep them quiet. The kidnappers escaped without awakening the cowhands in the bunkhouse."

Max said, "let's get geared up, we're already at least 6 hours behind. We need to make up time."

Their saddle bags were ready and all they needed was to pick up food for the trail. They were on their way within a half hour. Since their horses were fresh, they traveled at a fast trot for two hours before the first rest period. Thereafter they continued pushing till dark and continued into late evening at a careful slow walk. By midnight, they were exhausted and stopped for the evening. In setting up camp, they followed a well-established routine. Max took care of the horses, set up the saddles, saddlebags and bedroll in camp as Wes started a small cooking fire and prepared dinner. Taking nighttime camp security precautions, they both got a good night's sleep.

Meanwhile at the kidnapper's camp. The five men were in an uproar. Four men wanted to drink their whiskey and take advantage of the free victims. The leader of the men said, "there'll be no drinking and whoring tonight. You have to get some sleep because we have to push hard tomorrow. Our first delivery point is tomorrow night. This is a maiden enterprise, and if we are successful, we guarantee our future income. I cannot risk letting you animals loose on these hostages to mutilate them and ruin our packages. So, back off and go cool down in the river. By tomorrow night we'll deliver our hostages, get paid and head to town for celebrating."

The next morning, after a cold breakfast of jerky and cold coffee, Max asked what the plans were for the day. Wes explained, "to make your plans, pretend you are the kidnappers and what would you be thinking of doing."

"Guess, I'm too new at this, help me out."

"Well if I was the kidnappers working for a large crime syndicate, I would be expecting a rendezvous with a transferring team a full day's ride from here. This next team would have made plans to rent an entire box train at a watering stop, for the hostages, their horses and themselves. In other words, the kidnappers were the catch, grab, and go team. It's now time to hand their catch and get paid for their services."

Max picked up, "so if I read you right, we have to rescue the ladies before the transfer point, or they will be lost forever and so will our $10,000 fee."

"Right, so let's get on the road."

The duo moved right along and did some attentive tracking to keep on the proper trail. Max was beginning to improve his tracking abilities, even at the fast pace they were pushing their horses. Shortly after the third horse break, as they were turning a tight bend, the kidnappers were spotted some 200 yards across a flat prairie. The duo snuck into the trees and Wes said, "we're in trouble. There is our catch in the wide- open prairie. There is no way to sneak up on them and I suspect this is their last rest stop of the day before they meet with their connection. It's suicide for us to rush them and so this has all been for not."

Max thought a bit and finally said, "there is a way. I can pick them off one at a time with my scoped Win. 1876 on a tree rest."

"One problem, what do you do if, after the first hit, an outlaw puts his gun to a hostage's head?"

"I will shoot him in the head. The puff of smoke will appear a millisecond before the bullet is lodged in his brain. The sound will reach a few seconds later to roust the other kidnappers. By then, there will only be three more kidnappers remaining."

"Then what?"

"I keep picking them off till the remainder put their hands up, and you walk over there to handcuff them as I stay watching them thru the scoped rifle."

"Are you sure you can do this?"

"Of course, I can. The issue is whether it is ethically correct. Are we saving these ladies or are we executing their kidnappers?" Is it for saving the ladies or is it for the money?"

"Kill those evil psychopaths and save the ladies. If you don't want your share of the reward, give it away to charity. But do it now."

"I can live with that!"

Max decided to give them a warning shot which would also serve as a sighting shot. He aimed at a saddlebag next to the fire at an assumed 200 yards with a slight right to left breeze. He did the windage adjustment for a 5-mph wind and set his elevation on 200 yards. He aimed for the middle of the bag and hit dead center but low on the bottom of the bag. Without hesitating he made the elevation adjustment to compensate for the distance being likely in the 275-yard range.

The hit on the saddlebag made a loud clang since there must have been some metal cooking utensils in the bag.

Wes laughed when he saw the kidnappers jump out of their skin at the sound of a gun blast out of nowhere. He yelled, "we have you covered with a long-range rifle, give up or get picked off."

Four idiots blindly started shooting at the bushes with their pistols. Only one had the presence to grab his rifle with a range of 100 yards at best. That is when Max aimed center mass for the rifle shooter and pulled the trigger. The man was hit with a 350-grain bullet traveling at 1500 fps. On impact, he was lifted off the ground and thrown backwards several feet. He was dead before he hit the ground.

As expected, Waldo stepped to a hostage and put the barrel of his pistol to her head. He yelled out, "one more shot from you and I blow her brains out."

Max didn't even hesitate, he aimed for Waldo's face and pulled the trigger. The bullet entered his mouth and blew out the back of his skull. As he crumpled to the ground, the pistol fell out of his hand and hit the ground. On impact, it automatically fired, and Max saw another outlaw fall from an obvious gun shot to his leg. The last two lost their nerve to fight an invisible enemy at out of range distances. They both put their hands up, dropped their pistols, and yelled, "we give up, don't shoot."

When Wes and Max arrived at camp. The outlaw, hit in the leg by Waldo's pistol, was dead. He had obviously been hit in a major artery and bled to death, as marked by the large pool of blood on the ground. The first thing Max did was to remove the ropes from the hostages' wrists. He reassured them that they were now free and would be home by late tomorrow. One of the ladies asked, "after we go to the bushes, can we cook some dinner, we haven't had anything to eat since our kidnap?"

"Certainly, and Wes and I will join you."

While the ladies were cooking, the duo checked all the pockets and saddlebags. All they found was a half dozen boxes of 44 ammo and a 44 Webley Bulldog with a hip and shoulder holster. Max pilfered the Webley for future use in undercover work. The total amount of cash found amounted to a surprising $589 because Waldo had $500 in his pocket, a presumed down payment for his services. The two living outlaws were handcuffed with their hands behind their backs and one leg tied to a tree with a chain/ padlock.

The ladies outdid themselves, they cooked a great beef stew with three cans of beef and several cans of onions, potatoes and turnip. They also cooked biscuits and had plenty of coffee. For dessert they managed to make a peach cobbler out of two cans of peaches, flour and who knows what else.

During the evening, Wes talked with the two living kidnappers about trying to escape during the journey back to Laredo. Wes said, "it's very simple, if you try to escape, I'll shoot you dead since a kidnapper is wanted dead or alive."

"We won't try to escape, we want a lawyer and a trial. We believe we have a defense that will give us a short prison sentence instead of a hanging. That's why we gave up so easily."

The night was uneventful since Wes kept a fire going all night and with the extra bedrolls, the ladies were comfortable all night long. In the morning after a breakfast of beans, bacon and coffee, the caravan of ten horses took off for Laredo. Horses for three ladies, Wes and Max, two live outlaws manacled to their stirrups, and three dead bodies draped over and tied to the saddles.

Meanwhile, in Laredo, the ranching baron was holding a private meeting with the two other family members of the kidnapped victims. At the meeting was Sheriff Handy, a Texas Ranger Captain and members of the Cattlemen's Association. The cattle baron started speaking, "we have placed all our faith in two bounty hunters who were here in town at the time of the kidnapping. It's been four days, and nothing has been heard. I'm getting desperate and I think we should engage the Texas Rangers to cover San Antonio or Houston since our wives are likely lost in either city."

The Captain spoke up, "we don't have the manpower to cover both cities no matter how high the reward is. Since I think that San Antonio is too small and too close to Laredo to hide three local women, I say we flood Houston with all the manpower we can locate and as soon as possible. I would like to relocate my men as early as tonight."

Sheriff Handy, "now wait, you know Wes and Max. They are good trackers, gunfighters and dedicated to every job. They always get results. I think you should give them another full day before you change tactics especially since the Captain suspects their destination is Houston."

As everyone started talking at the same time, no one noticed that the caravan had arrived at the sheriff's office. The deputy told Wes what was going on at the Palace Saloon and Wes took off to join the party. West slammed into the batwing doors and yelled out, "I need a beer."

Jaws dropped and everyone stepped outside to see three beautiful ladies still sitting on their horses. The reunion was emotional, but the three ranchers never forgot their wives' rescuers. One of them said to Max, "come to the bank in the morning and you'll have your reward--and thanks for saving my wife."

The next day was spent identifying the three dead outlaws and sending for verification of bounty rewards. The two live ones had no bounty, Waldo had a $500 reward and the two dead outlaws had each a $250 bounty—all for rustling and bank robbery.

Disregarding the $89 in petty cash, this caper had netted $1,000 in bounty rewards, $500 cash in Waldo's pocket, $300 for pistols and rifles, $500 for eight saddled horses and $10,000 from the ranchers.

Max stood there holding almost $5,000 in cash money as he was filling out a deposit slip at the bank. West knew Max was hesitating and before he could say something. Wes whispered, "Accept it and deposit it before you change your mind. You can always be charitable in the future once you develop or find a worthwhile cause."

The next week, Wes and Max enjoyed the luxury of city living in a high-class hotel with its own gambling casino. They walked the streets and got familiar with the tonsorial shops, mercantiles, saloons, and the many Mexican and American diners. It was in one of the local diners that Sheriff Handy came to see them with a problem.

"I just got a telegram from the Texas Ranger Captain. It appears that a Colonel of the Mexican army deserted and brought eight men with him to form a band of bandits. The problem is that they are operating on both the American and Mexican side of the river, but doing their kidnapping on the American side, of course."

"So how does that affect us?"

"They are pillaging and raiding all the small settlements for a hundred mile between Laredo and your old Valley. They are killing the inhabitants randomly, burning the buildings, and leaving with as many women as they can carry, doubling on horseback. Of course, by the time the Texas Rangers respond, the Colonel and his band are far into Mexico and heading for Monterrey, Mexico, where they sell their hostages. To make it worse, these American women are raped and ravaged all the way to their destination."

Wes asks, "how far is Monterrey?"

"From Laredo 150 miles, from the Valley 130 miles and from the midpoint between Laredo and the Valley, as the river bends into Mexico, 80 miles—all cross country without roads."

"Who is putting up the reward and how much is it?"

"The state of Texas thru the Texas Rangers. All because, the Texas Rangers and not allowed into Mexico to chase the Colonel down. The reward is $2,000 for the Colonel and $500 for any of his band, which I'm told is up to twenty."

"And you expect Max and I to catch this bandit and his army?"

"Yes!"

"How?"

"Guerrilla warfare in his own country. Ambush, long range shooting, steal his horses, burn his supplies, poison his water supply, rock slides, set up bear traps in their camps at night—are you getting my drift? Any kind of lethal mischief to dwindle his numbers till you are comfortable with a frontal attack."

Wes says, "that's a new twist, might be quite enjoyable and profitable."

"I agree, I especially like the bear traps. Sounds like the appropriate justice for these animals."

"Ok, Sheriff, we'll seriously think on it a few days and get back to you."

Sheriff Handy already knew what their answer would be

***

CHAPTER 6— Becoming a legend

It didn't take long for Wes and Max to decide that this guerilla warfare was worth a trial. So, they bought two pack horses and loaded them with tools of the trade: coal oil, wolf traps, bear traps, laxatives, loco weed, syrup of ipecac, dynamite and snare wire.

The next day, Sheriff Handy told Wes that the Colonel and his raiders had been terrorizing the homesteaders half way to the Valley. They had been terrorizing homesteaders, stealing horses and kidnapping any woman that came in their paths—irrelevant of the age.

Two days later, Wes and Max arrived in the area where the Colonel had hit yesterday. They had stolen eleven horses and eight women. A couple days ago it was four horses and three women. It was the consensus of the local men that with an army of twenty toadies, they would continue pillaging till they had more hostages and horses for sale in Monterrey.

The Texas Rangers were patrolling the entire

river border, but they had no idea where the Colonel would hit next. Wes and Max elected to camp just outside a small settlement—on the Mexican side of the river. That way, they could saddle their riding and pack horses in a hurry and be on the trail. Their camp was well hidden across a commonly used river crossing area.

That night around midnight, shooting was heard to the northwest and lasted for a half hour. The bandits must have burned the entire settlement since a red glow was visible in the sky. The boys immediately closed camp and waited by the river ford. To their astonishment, some thirty riders appeared, of which were ten women of different ages tied to their saddle horns.

Wes said, "looks like they are all heading to their camp and pick up the other hostages and horses. It looks like they have a full haul and will be heading to Monterrey. It's now or never Max. What say you?"

"It's clear to me, they have at least twenty of our women and young girls. Time to put an end to these depredations. We have the tools and the courage to do it. So, off we go, heh!"

That first night was spent gathering intelligence. Max was using his 50X binoculars by sunup. He reported: nineteen American women, twenty Mexican locals and the Colonel. They had no wagons but had many pack saddles on the ground for carrying supplies. There were some one hundred or more horses.

Wes said, "that's too many horses to escort these hostages. They will pair a horse to each hombre, woman and pack saddle. The remainder will be a separate remuda that will be following the caravan of hostages. We'll be able to attack each one separately."

The next morning, the duo was waiting for the caravan to pass. They were well hidden in a thick grove of trees. Max had his scoped Win 76 ready and Wes was sitting on his horse waiting for the remuda to arrive. Half an hour later, the remuda was escorted by three Mexican bandits. Wes waited till the remuda got to within fifty yards. He then threw a lit stick of dynamite at the horses. It landed twenty-five yards away and scattered every horse to kingdom-come. The three bandits were trying to locate where the dynamite came from when they spotted Wes.

The shooting started and Wes shot the lead man out of the saddle, but Max had the other two covered and both went down without ever firing a shot. The bandits were left to the predators, their horses released to the wild without their bridles or saddles. The Mexican firearms were destroyed and the only thing that was saved was the three saddlebags as proof of their demise. It was clear that the Colonel had heard the dynamite blast but did not know its long-term implications.

That same night, the duo left their horses 400 yards from the Colonel's camp, put on their moccasins and walked to camp after midnight with the tools of the trade. Entering the camp all the bandits were asleep including the hostage guard. Wes got one woman's attention, motioned to the men's bushes, and showed the lady a bear trap. The woman acknowledged by crude sigh language, that the ladies used their own private area in the bushes. The duo then proceeded to lay out a large patch of wolf traps and one bear trap on the trail, ahead of the wolf traps. Before departing, they left their greeting card, Max placed the three saddlebags of the remuda guards next to the wolf trap patch. They then stepped aside and waited some 200 yards away to see the result of their mischief, through their binoculars.

The first outlaw awoke at daybreak and rushed to the bushes. Suddenly, a loud metal snap was followed by a penetrating scream of total horror. Every bandit rushed to see what had happened, only to see their friend laying on the ground, his boot cut in half, with a massive foot trap holding on to an obviously broken leg being held by strips of flesh.

Every man stepped up to release the bear trap. As they approached the trapped man, they started mulling around the man trying to decide how to open the trap. Suddenly, the men started stepping on the wolf traps. Again, their friends came to help them and more wolf traps started going off. It was mayhem at its best and at least four men were yelling a chilling sound of guerilla justice.

The next morning, the Colonel had a dilemma. One man had nearly bled to death and three others could not walk with their foot and leg injuries. These men could not continue the seventy more miles to Monterrey and so, the four men had to leave the Colonel to seek medical care nearby. Max was watching thru his binoculars and said, "I see four riders off on their own, heading north. That makes it seven down."

Wes added, "look at the Colonel, he's holding up the three saddlebags and you can tell, not only does he recognize them, but he's one unhappy puppy!"

The next night, mischief continued. Fortunately for the duo, these bandits drank heavily after dinner and usually fell asleep totally drunk. Wes and Max again entered the camp around 2AM. Wes motioned to the same lady to watch. As they added a powder to the can of new coffee and a liquid to several bottles of whiskey.

By morning, the Colonel felt confident that the depredations against them were over, and if he pushed the caravan hard today, they would be in Monterrey by tomorrow. After a full breakfast and several pots of coffee, the camp was closed and only water was given to the hostages for another day. To boost morale, several of his men were allowed to service themselves on older women before leaving camp. The young maidens were left untouched since they brought in more money if they were virgins.

Two hours on the trail, several men started complaining of belly cramps. Man, after man, they would jump off their horses and squat on the spot to relieve themselves before they soiled their britches. The women couldn't help but start laughing. Suddenly, the Colonel himself had to run away to privacy, but didn't make it in time. He was furious as he ordered a change of clothes.

The duo watched the turmoil from 300 yards. Max was amazed at the site covered with feces and soiled britches. He added, "those idiots are drinking whiskey instead of water. Some of them are going to get the ipecac. Oh Well!"

When the Colonel half recovered from sitting on a log all day to keep up with the explosive urge to relieve himself, he asked who the guard was last night that allowed some Gringoes to poison the coffee since none of the women were affected. The guard was found, but he was busy vomiting as well a having the backdoor trots. To be shot would have been a blessing.

The vomiting was continuous. With the combination of the two, no one could hold water down and many were going into shock. Being in shock did not stop the eliminations, and many men lay in their own body fluids. The shock was often fatal and by the next day, five more men were seen being buried.

The Colonel had watched the hostages and quickly realized that one woman had become their leader. He had his brutal man select her and ordered him to beat her to near unconsciousness.

Wes and Max had seen what was going on. When the bear of a man tore off this lady's clothes and dropped his own britches, Max went for his rifle. Wes says, "he's straddling her, spreading her legs and he's going to rape her. "Take him out, now!" Using his scoped rifle free style, he knew the scope settings would shoot low. So, he aimed at his chest and fired. Wes saw the impact. It was low abdomen almost in the hip area, and low enough to amputate his manhood. The man looked at his mutilated body and rolled off his victim to writhe about before bleeding to death.

The shot forced the mess of dirty Mexicans to reach for their rifles. Yet, they were out of range and no target could be found. Max said, "six more dead and only seven to go plus the Colonel!"

That same night, the chosen mischief seemed to turn the gang into mutiny. During the late night, the duo crept into camp. Pouring a gallon of coal oil over the stacked food supplies, they lit it, ran into the trees and left the empty gallon pail for everyone to see. On the can was a note, "from your gringo admirers."

From 50 yards away, they saw a bunch of Mexicans try to put out the fire or pull out some supplies. As this was happening, the duo let off four shots from their sawed-off shotguns sending hundreds of #4 pellets downrange—not able to kill but certainly enough to cause pain from imbedded pellets in the skin.

As the Mexicans were hiding behind their saddles, the duo quickly ran to their horses and left the area. Meanwhile, the Colonel realized that these pellets had to re removed or infection would set in. He convinced the abused hostage leader to make an incision and probe with small forceps to remove the pellets. As an incentive for her not to knife his men, the Colonel held a knife against the nose of a young girl, with the warning, "attack my men and I cut her nose off."

With dawn approaching, Wes said, "tomorrow is the last day before the caravan gets to Monterrey. We've pruned their numbers, but we are still left with seven hombres—and not one is in a good mood."

"Time for a long-range assault followed by a face to face gunfight and rescue. Guess we'll keep the loco weed and wire snares for another caper."

The duo rode ahead of the caravan and chose a unique location on a cliff overlooking the trail below. The yardage appeared to be 300 yards and Max set his scope accordingly. They waited almost two hours before the caravan arrived. Max took careful aim and in a matter of seconds, quickly dispatched three of the bandits. The remainder had taken refuge behind boulders but could not find a target within range of their rifles.

With only four men left, the Colonel had his handgun drawn and was watching over the hostages. For a long time, nothing was happening. Suddenly, on their quiet moccasins, the duo appeared at the back of the waiting Mexicans. Wes yells out, "put your hands up or you're all dead.".

The bandits knew that they would hang from a kidnapping guilty verdict in either Mexico or the US. They had no choice but to fight it out. Without any hesitation the four Mexicans turned and pointed their rifles at Wes and Max. The sound of four shotgun shots was deafening and the acrid smell of burnt gunpowder made every eye water. When the smoke cleared, the Colonel was the only bandit left standing. With his cocked pistol at the dominant woman's head, he spoke up, "as an ex-Colonel, I request to be treated respectfully as an officer who has the right to a trial in his own country where I have a defense.

If you don't accept my terms, shoot me but I will take this young woman with me."

Wes looked at Max and said, "take care of this piece of crap."

Max drew, fired and placed the bullet direct in the Colonel's groin. The protective reflex of holding your groin when hit in the testicles was the same drive when shot in the groin. The Colonel thrust his hands to his crotch and the cocked pistol was thrown to the ground without firing.

Wes picked the Colonel by the lapel and stood him up as he landed a straight roundhouse punch to the man's mouth. He then said, you are the lowest of life, a real dirt bag. You kidnap women, burn settlements, kill innocent people, allow your men to rape the prisoners, and worse of all, you ordered this woman beat to unconsciousness. For this last reason, you are going to violently die at my hands."

The beating started, punch after punch to the face and head till there was no life left in the body. The dominant woman stepped up, placed her hands on Wes's shoulders and said. "this animal is now in front of his maker, and you can now rest.

Thank you for saving our lives. My name by the way is Meg Morrow."

The men were all buried with their disabled firearms. Collected from the Colonel's saddlebags was $600 which was likely pay for his twenty men--$30 per man to kidnap another human. Wes handed the money to Meg and asked that she distribute the funds according to need.

After preparing a fine dinner, the ladies finally were able to share their misfortune with the duo. Meg pointed out that several of the older ladies were at risk of getting pregnant from the sexual abuse they had endured. The consensus was that any pregnant woman would have the help of the others in raising the child or even adopting it if necessary. Later, Max told Meg in private that, if any lady had this misfortune, he would help to financially support the raising of the child. Meg was surprised and said, "how can you afford to pay for such expenses?"

"I have an account made up of bounty rewards that will pay for some of these expenses, and I'm glad to do it."

Two days later, the rescued ladies arrived in town and went straight to the sheriff's office. The women verified that Wes and Max had eliminated the Colonel and his men, and they were due the $500 reward for each of twenty men, and the bounty on the Colonel. Nothing was said about the men seeking medical care from animal traps.

Next was the reunion. Parents and husbands were arriving. There was much joy and tears to go around. Most husbands knew of their wives' situation. Fortunately, it was clear that these couples would find a way to go forward and put this nightmare behind them. Wes was watching the reunion with Meg.

A couple was seen talking a bit separated from the others. Suddenly, the man slapped his wife and walked away. Meg went up to the stricken lady while Wes went to confront the husband. He stopped the man and said, "you just abandoned your wife. Don't you know that she didn't choose to be raped? Are you so stupid that you don't understand your wife is the victim?"

"Mind your own business."

"I have to make it my business since someone has to speak for your wife. This is what you deserve." Wes drew his right arm back and smacked him, with all his might, with a straight right punch to the mouth. The man went down, but Wes lifted him off the ground by the shirt and pummeled him two more times.

Meg said, "that's enough Wes. Now being toothless, everyone will remember this day, and how he lost all his front teeth." Max saw the entire event and knew that he could do something to bring long term justice to this unfortunate lady.

Two weeks later, Sheriff Handy succeeded in obtaining the bounty money from the slow Texas state coffers. The state vouchers amounted to $12,000. What the duo never knew was that upon their departure, the families and husbands had amassed another $3,000 in private rewards.

Max had taken upon himself to help the abandoned housewife named Cindy McShane. He brought her to a mercantile and bought her a new wardrobe. Next, he bought her a Webley Bulldog pistol for self-defense, and paid for a year's stay in a local boarding house. He gave her $50 in cash and started a $400 bank account in her name. The last thing he did was to bring her to a lawyer to start divorce proceedings. When the lawyer realized this was a well-dressed, sharp and educated lady, he offered her a job as his law clerk. Max left the lawyer's office with a crying woman on his arm. Cindy finally stopped blubbering and said, "to the end of my new life, I will never forget your generosity and I hope I can help someone someday—thank you."

Weeks passed and the duo refused to take on several bank robbery jobs. Instead, they decided to stop the human trafficking from Laredo. The San Antonio crime syndicate had failed to get new women by using local hoodlums. Now, they were sending existing outlaw gangs to Laredo to kidnap women and bring them cross country to San Antonio, where some were placed in the local brothels and some went cross country to Houston. The use of the railroad proved to be a loss for the syndicate since the Texas Rangers were patrolling and disbanding the kidnappers.

Sheriff Handy proved to be a perfect source for information. Any new apparent gangs would be spotted by him or his deputies and reported to the duo. Whenever there was a kidnapping that was reported to the sheriff, the duo would match the day to whenever the gangs were not in saloons. After a half dozen kidnappings, it became obvious that the hostages were being kept in some abandoned house outside of town.

In addition, a certain gang of four men would spend evenings in one saloon—the Golden

Bucket. The strange thing was that the four men were never the same. It became clear that two men would remain in camp or in their abandoned house to guard the prisoners while the others drank and whored in the saloon.

After putting together this revelation, and with two more kidnappings from distant ranches, it was decided that something had to be done to rescue the prisoners and arrest this entire gang. That evening the word was passed around that the Texas Rangers were coming to town to put an end to these kidnappings. Hearing this, the gang got up and left the saloon. Wes and Max were ready and followed them to their hideout. They arrived at a small ranch house off the beaten path. Being close to daybreak, they decided to wait till morning to set up their rescuing scheme.

The duo's intuition had been correct. Today was the day kidnappers would begin moving their prisoners to San Antonio. During the night, the duo moved into the barn where a dozen horses were housed. They elected to wait by the door with each a shovel in hand. As expected, two outlaws were heading for the barn. They never got past the door without coming in contact with a swinging steel wall. The unconscious scoundrels were bound, gagged and hid away. Half an hour later a scout was sent to the barn while complaining, "you idiots, you're suppose to saddle horses, not drink wh……" He never finished his words before joining his buddies.

The fourth man came out with his pistol drawn. As he entered the barn, Wes apparently hit him too hard because he fell to the ground--dead on impact. Max said, "I believe the kidnappers know something is amiss. Time for us to show our faces and have a showdown."

Stepping to the porch, Wes called out the kidnappers. "We know you are in there. Step out or we'll come in."

Coming out were two vile looking creatures. One was holding a gun to the head of a frightened young girl, and the other was holding a double barrel shotgun with both mule ears cocked back. One outlaw spoke, "we want two horses and we'll leave the girl a mile down the road. It's either that or I shoot both of you with this shotgun and my partner will kill the girl."

Wes looked at Max and they both realized that standing on the ground with the outlaws on the porch, they were actually two feet lower than the outlaws. A shot to the head would allow the bullet to hit high at the house and certainly above the head of the prisoners in the house. Wes just nodded and Max took over.

"We can't do that, you are under arrest. If you don't surrender you will both die."

"Them are big words for someone without a gun in hand and looking down the barrel of a scatter gun."

Realizing that further discussion was useless, Max drew and fired twice. The outlaw holding the uncocked pistol was shot in the right eye and fell to the floor like a rock in water. The shotgun man lost his right hand as the bullet impacted his hand at the wrist. The outlaw dropped the shotgun, screamed in pain and horror, and tried to squeeze his right wrist to stop the spraying of blood. All the prisoners were safe.

On the ride back to Laredo, Wes asked Max, "why didn't you kill the man holding the shotgun?"

"Because we are not executioners. I know it's easier and safer to bring a man draped over the saddle. By constantly doing this, we get the public to see us as harvesters of wanted bodies for money. I would rather give the impression that we always save our victims and bring in some outlaws dead and some alive, but not well treated. This last batch had two dead, three outlaws with skull fractures and one without a hand.

A week later three things happened. A local newspaper was labeling the duo as legends in their time. So far on several kidnapping capers, every victim was rescued alive. Second, Wes had fallen in love with Meg and was talking of retiring or taking a job as a deputy for Sheriff Handy. Third, Sheriff McFarlane in his home town was having health issues that required complicated surgery in San Antonio. Max was asked to take the sheriff's job on a temporary basis. At the same time, he got a telegram from his dad announcing that Jenna was getting married. It was hoped that he could join them for the wedding.

Without any doubt, Max would be at his sister's wedding. At the same time, by becoming the local sheriff, it was an opportunity to visit with his family and get to know his new brother-in-law. Little did he realize that this new brother-in-law had a sister that would capture his own heart and provide a new direction to his life.

***

BOOK THREE

MAX AND SYLVIA

CHAPTER 7—Building a foundation

"My family tells me you are quite a pistol."

"Well, I've been called all sorts of names, but that's a new one. Care to explain?"

"That you're well educated, driven, motivated, and have a pleasant personality."

"Oh well, that is better than what I presumed you meant!"

Max thought—*I wonder if she realizes that she is down-right gorgeous with ample female curves—even if she hides them in men's britches and work shirt. I bet if she dropped the pony tail, she would be some beauty!*

"Jenna tells me you are planning a commercial vegetable growing enterprise. How far along are you?"

"We have at least 100 acres cultivated, fertilized and ready for planting. Dad and Brian have erected all six of our windmills and with the Mexican workers, we now are filling six holding ponds with the attached windmill modification to pump water from the river. Brian is now digging irrigation ditches by using an adapter to his horse drawn plow. Dad is checking the elevation to guarantee gravity drainage to accommodate row and plot flooding."

"That's a great start, where are you along in this beginning?"

"Jenna and I have been planting individual seeds in our own potting soil mixture. The seeds are planted in glass tubes for germination and later will be transplanted to clay pots for further maturing in the heated glass house, before planting outside."

"Really, what vegetable varieties are you seeding this time of year?"

"We are filling the greenhouse with a winter crop of six hardy vegetables: cabbage, cauliflower, brussels-sprouts, peppers, broccoli, and turnip. Each vegetable has three separated plantings to allow harvesting over a longer period. When all planted, we'll have nearly 2500 plants growing and maturing in the greenhouse."

"That means transplanting 2500 fragile seedlings to clay pots. Along with maintaining a temperature above freezing and watering them regularly."

"You have the gist of it, that's my work till the

holidays. Then we hope to have a mild winter and we'll start planting the potted plants."

"How will you do that? Not 2500 plants manually?"

"No, we have designed a horse drawn planter. It has two seats. The front seat is for the horse driver. The rear seat is for the operator. The machine makes a furrow, the operator picks up a recently watered pot from the right tray, pulls out the plant and pushes it in the furrow. The clay pot is placed on the left tray for future use. Two wings bury the transplant and rollers gently packs the earth. The operator takes another potted plant and the process continues. Of note, the driver controls the horse's pace and establishes the space between plants. Brian will drive the horses and I will be the operator."

"Yes Ma'am, it's nice to see a plan come together. You appear very secure with your schedule."

"Well, I've had a good training at the University and this element of olericulture is just the beginning. The spring planting season starts the real work and all of my family will be involved, including Jenna. Now that's enough about me and my dream. What about you? I have heard that you were a successful bounty hunter who had now become a legendary savior of kidnapped women. Please tell me your story."

"Well my story is rather simple. I left home at an early age when my parents realized I was not meant to be an animal feed grower. I went to work for a gunsmith and learned the trade as well as the proficiency with all firearms. I practiced shooting for years till I became lightning fast with a Colt and a marksman with a long-range rifle."

"One day, I had the opportunity to go after bank robbers with an experienced bounty hunter, and I've been with him ever since. We were fortunate, by mixing his experience and my proficiency with firearms, we were successful and made a lot of money. Actually, more money than we deserved. I remedied that inequity by giving some of my income to the needy victims of injustice."

"This past year, Laredo and its surrounding settlements, have been plagued with the evil of human trafficking. Innocent women have become victims and the law has not rescued them for a multitude of reasons. It was Sheriff Handy in Laredo who convinced us to try to rescue a kidnapped group of women. Well to make a long-complicated story short, we were successful repeatedly without loosing a single victim to the outlaws—and that's where the legend came from, thanks to the exaggerated writings of a newspaper reporter."

Currently, my partner has fallen in love with a kidnapped victim we liberated, and he is taking a vacation from bounty hunting. I had nothing planned when Sheriff McFarlane asked me to replace him for six months while he sought complicated surgery out of town. In a nut shell, that's my story."

Without warning, the music started. Sylvia adds, "oh no, we were supposed to mix and talk to all the guests before dancing started."

"Instead of talking niceties to many people, we were able to talk and get to know each other. Now that was not a waste of time!"

Sylvia agreed but wondered how the remainder of the evening would go. She wanted to know more about Max Adams, as Max said, "the music tune sounds like a two-step and the couples are doing the Texas two-step. Would you join me in a dance if I promise to keep my feet off your toes?"

"I would love to, but you'll have to help me since I'm a bit stale with this social activity."

The dance started and both were rather stiff and clumsy. With persistence and allowing their guard down, they clearly started moving with the beat and started enjoying the dance. Most important, they were both feeling the result of touching and enjoying every moment.

As is usually the case, not everyone was dancing. There were spectators for whatever reason. One of the spectators was a Mexican Nobleman and a mega Rancher, Marquis Juan Guerra. This invitee was a large customer of Elmer Adams who always placed a large order of hay and oats for his animals.

> The Marquis hailed his segundo and said, "see the young dancing maiden wearing a red dress and black belt. She has her dark hair in the 'American pony tail' and is dancing with the young policeman. Find out who she is and whatever you can about her. Now, and get back to me."

The young couple dance another dance which was much slower. The closeness was more obvious and more sensual. At the end of the dance, they walked to the side of the dance floor while holding hands. It was Max who realized they were holding hands in public and let go of Sylvia's hand. Sylvia would have none of it. She moved her hand over and Max gladly grabbed it.

Max leaned over and said, "when something feels right, then it's usually right." Sylvia didn't speak but hid a smile as she gently squeezed Max's hand. The dancing resumed, and the two danced the evening away, yet finding something to talk about during the musicians' rest periods.

Meanwhile, the segundo returned to the Marquis. "The American maiden is the college educated daughter of Grant Cassidy. a rancher from Dallas. He and his family are neighbors and friends of Elmer Adams. The Cassidys are starting a vegetable commercial enterprise. The maiden's name is Sylvia, she is not married, but has the reputation of being strong minded." The Marquis nodded and waved his segundo away.

Eventually, the evening came to an end. Max and Sylvia went for a walk, hand in hand, and talked about the coming week. Sylvia said, "the wedding is in three days and I'll be busy with all the preparations."

Max added, "and I need to get reacquainted with the town and all of its merchants. I have a deputy which will give me relief from the doldrums of the job, and I'd like to call on you after the wedding. Is that possible?"

"Yes, I'd like that very much."

Max escorted Sylvia to her home. When they arrived, they brought her horse to the barn to be fed, watered and unsaddled. Before leaving, Max leaned forward and gave Sylvia a soft kiss and said, "it's been an enlightening evening and I look forward to more of the same."

Sylvia just stood there, almost mummified, with a thousand old and new thoughts going thru her mind. Without fully comprehending her behavior, she put her hands around Max's neck and returned a rather passionate and prolonged kiss. After the kiss, she turned and walked to her house.

Max stood there and was a bit out of sorts as he watched her walk away. Max found himself in uncontrolled arousal and had to walk his horse for a mile before he got up and slowly sat in the saddle. He must have been daydreaming because the next thing he remembered was arriving at the sheriff's office in town. Sitting in the saddle, he thought, *meeting and spending the evening with that special lady certainly had affected his senses. He had become less alert of his surroundings, and that placed a lawman and bounty hunter at risk of catching a bullet. He rationalized that the encounter was new to him and probably accounted for his lack of self-preservation. A better disciplined approach was needed, since not calling on Sylvia was not in the cards.*

At the same time, Sylvia was trying to get some sleep when she started second guessing herself. She thought, "*was I too forward? Did I act to aggressive? Did I appear to be a dominatrix? She realized that she had never had any romantic contact with any man, and although she was still a virgin, she didn't want her physical condition to become a lifelong disease. She wanted her career and she wanted to fall in love with an equal, to raise a family and run a business—Sylvia's dream.*

The next three days were very busy. Sylvia

helped modifying Jenna's dress, arranging a luncheon at Kate's diner, and shopping for her own dress. To her dismay, Bess had decided that Jenna should have a bridesmaid. Since Sylvia was the only female of significance to Jenna, she was forcibly recruited. In the end, she would be officially accompanied by Brian's best man, Max.

In all of Sylvia's life, she had never had to wait for want. Now all she could think about was seeing Max again and verifying that their beginning encounter was not a discard-able fling.

During the same three days, Max bought a dressed-up suit with matching vest. He even bought a tie and a white boiled shirt for the occasion. He didn't understand why Brian needed a best man since the marriage license witnesses were Grant and Elmer. Max made it clear that he didn't want to be attached to the bridesmaid which was the tradition of the time. Brian understood his resistance and put an end to it by saying that Sylvia was the bridesmaid.

The three days went by quickly as time was spent learning the routine of making rounds in town and greeting old acquaintances. By habit, he studied the wanted posters regularly, in case some of these outlaws showed up in town. The

Valley was often the last stop before escaping into Mexico. For that reason, every evening round included a good look inside the local saloons.

The night before the wedding, Max was finishing his evening rounds in the busiest saloon in town. Stepping in, he would have a beer to help him sleep the night before the wedding. Taking his beer to a table where the town doctor was enjoying an evening brandy, Max saw a man that he was certain had a face on a wanted poster. After a short visit with the doctor, Max got up and walked by the suspected outlaw.

Within striking distance, Max swung the empty heavy beer mug on top of the outlaw's head and knocked him flat on the table. Several patrons were stunned, and one said, "why did you buffalo this man?"

"Because, I don't risk my life to be kind or to save an outlaw. This man is wanted for several murders of innocent men just like yourselves. We'll all be safer to bring him to jail unconscious versus at gunpoint."

***

CHAPTER 8— Calling on Sylvia

The wedding was held in the United Methodist Church in town. The guests included all the neighboring homesteaders and most of the merchants in town. Some sixty people were seated as Brian and Max stood next to the minister and waited for the bride and bridesmaid. As the organist started to play "here comes the bride," Sylvia appeared first and started down the aisle. Max could not believe his eyes. Her black hair was down to her shoulders and she was wearing a floor length light blue gown with a "hobble skirt"—not a tent type dress for everyday use. Brian heard Max softly say, "my God, she looks like a tall goddess."

Following Sylvia, Jenna appeared in her white bride's gown escorted by her dad. The minister did not dawdle and got thru the marriage vows. Max and Sylvia spent the entire proceedings staring at each other and came out of their trances as the minister said, "you may now kiss the bride!"

The recession allowed the best man and

bridesmaid to walk out of the church hand in hand. A reception line was set up outside the church. Max and Sylvia were standing side by side and Sylvia was introducing her friends and family to Max and vice versa. Max thought, "*how ironic, the way we are introducing each-other's friends and family, we are acting like husband and wife—just like Brian and Jenna were doing in the reception line.*

In the reception line was the Nobleman Marquis with his attendants waiting next to the line. It was Max who introduced him to Sylvia, as one of his dad's business associates. The Marquis shook Sylvia's hand and merely said, "pleased to meet you," and moved on. The Marquis moved away from the reception line, but his segundo knew more would come of this encounter.

Kates Diner did a magnificent job of catering a hot chicken pie dinner in the parish hall. The dessert was the lemon wedding cake with tea and coffee. After the tables were cleaned, a dance followed. No one asked Max or Sylvia to dance. It was clear to everyone that these two were already becoming an item of significance.

During an intermission, Max and Sylvia went for some private time outside. Sylvia started, "for the past three days, when I didn't hear or see you, I wondered if I had not overdone my eagerness to return your kiss. Actually, I convinced myself that I had, and that I had alienated you a bit?"

Sylvia, that is nonsense. For the past three days, I have been walking in a daze. I cannot keep my mind on the job. All I think is about you and how I want to be with you. So, during my three-day training, I sent a message, by Gary Sweeney, to Wes in Laredo. I offered him Sheriff McFarlane's job for the next six months and he accepted. He and his girlfriend will be here tonight, and I reserved them a room in Aunt Jenny's Boarding House."

"So, what are you going to do with all your free time?"

"Well with Brian and Jenna being on their week's honeymoon in town at the Winslow Hotel, I figured you needed a helper in the greenhouse. That will allow me to kill two birds with one stone."

"And what would that achieve?"

"I would get to learn about olericulture and your business dream, and we would get to know each other. Hopefully, some developments might be bound to happen, heh."

They went back in the hall once the music restarted. They danced regularly and were in their own private world. Whenever they rested, they sat at a table and held hands. Very few words were said but many emotions were shared.

> Meanwhile, the Marquis was watching this beautiful maiden in an elegant floor length light blue straight dress. He was mesmerized by her demeanor while dancing. Despite the fact that the dress was tight around her bosom and other curves, she managed to maneuver the fast dances with grace. When he saw her in private communications with the Adams boy, he became envious. When the envy turned to jealousy, he ordered his segundo to bring the carriage around, and left the celebration without a departing good wish to the bride and groom.

As all great events come to an end, the wedding day was over, and the newlyweds departed for their week's honeymoon in town at the Winslow

Hotel. Max escorted her to the buggy. Sylvia said, "it's not modest for a lady to lift her dress above the knees to step up into the buggy."

Max never hesitated, he placed his hands behind her thighs and low back and said. "Ma'am, you are a real mole."

While still in his arms, she asked, "what do you mean a mole?"

"When you entered the church, no one ever thought that a farm girl dressed in pants could ever clean up so well. You are gorgeous, your dress brought out your personality, and every woman and man at that wedding was pleasantly surprised."

"I don't care about the others, I care about what you thought?"

With Sylvia still in his arms, he kissed her gently but passionately.

"Is there any doubt in your mind how I feel about you?"

"No, I guess not. Guess you can put me down, heh?"

Max unceremoniously drops and plops her down in the buggy's seat. When Sylvia recovered, she added, "wow, that works as good as a cold bath in turning off the passion"—as they both started to laugh. On the way back to Sylvia's home, the passion rekindled, and Sylvia was not bashful in expressing her feelings. By the time they got home, Max was again in a bad shape, and had to walk his horse a bit before riding up in the saddle.

Max thought, *"one of these days, soon, when she gets me into this condition, I won't have to walk my horse home."*

***

The next day, Sylvia was waiting for Max in the greenhouse with a fresh pot of coffee on the heating stove, and a fresh batch of bearpaw pastries. She knew she had met her soulmate and equal, and hoped the week working with Max would convince him of the same. Max arrived, put up his horse in the barn, unsaddled and gave him hay, and walked over to the greenhouse with a gift in hand for Sylvia.

"This is for you."

"What did I do to deserve this?"

"That dress! Open it."

"A small pistol with a shoulder holster and a hip holster. Why."

"Because, every man in town now knows that you are some new- found beauty. Human nature as it is, you need to be able to protect yourself. During the week, on breaks, I will train you in self-defense with that pistol."

"I thought a shotgun was adequate protection."

"Yes, when in your hands. However, an attack always comes unannounced, and the only defense you have is what is in your hands—that's either air or a gun."

"Ok, have some coffee and bearpaws before we start."

Max was put on the detail of mixing the ingredients to make potting soil. The instructions were clear, and he would make a batch that would take Sylvia at least two days to use up. His second job involved watering all the plants. Fortunately, they had installed a "point well" and hand pump in the greenhouse, making the filling of the sprinkling bucket an easy job. Using the sprinkling bucket was not easy and was time consuming. Glass tubes were either over watered or under watered. The sprinkler was cumbersome.

While he turned with the bucket, he accidentally tipped it over Sylvia's head. Sylvia gasped at the sudden cold water over her head. Max started laughing but quickly saw what the water had done to her shirt. Sylvia looked at what Max was staring at and saw her nipples had puckered-up and protruded thru the shirt and chemise. Sylvia never missed a step and said, "If you wanted to see my nipples, all you had to do was ask and I would have avoided the cold bath!"

Max turned red faced and was about to apologize when he retorted, "that was payback for placing me in a predicament, after kissing, that forced me to walk next to my horse."

Sylvia thought, *"well I could say that I won't kiss passionately again but decided not to. It was best to just smile and move on."*

Getting back to the issue, Max added, "this sprinkler on a bucket is not going to work, too much water is falling on your tables and missing the plants. I'm going to design something more efficient and quicker. Where are your dad's replacement parts for the implements?"

"In the implement shed's storage cabinet."

Max opened the cabinet, rummaged around and found three parts that would work. Back at the greenhouse he built a high and narrow table on wheels that was two feet higher than the table holding the plants. He then took the sprinkler bucket, left the sprinkler in place, bored a hole in the bucket lower sidewall, added an adapter, attached a flexible ½ inch by 3-foot hose, and placed a stop-cock at the distal end.

Back in the green house, Sylvia looked at his contraption. The bucket, placed on the high table, was draining water by gravity. Max had the stop-cock adjusted to allow moving from one glass tube to another without stopping. For the transplants in the clay pots, the stop-cock was opened to increase the flow of water between each clay pot. Again, Max did not have to stop watering between each clay pot.

Sylvia was watching, shaking her head but smiling. She clapped her hands and finally spoke, "that's a marvelous invention that will allow uniform watering and save many manhours. Guess you're forgiven for puckering some of my body parts."

After the watering was done on 2000 plants, Max helped Sylvia on the next batch of the last 1000 plants. Max was adding potting soil to the fixed level in the glass tubes and preparing more potting soil when needed. Working thru lunch, they quit working at 3PM in order to start their shooting training.

Sylvia knew about gun safety and needed a short lesson on the operation of the pistol. She was pleased to find that this Bulldog was both a single and double action pistol. The double action meant that she only needed to pull the trigger to make it fire--compared to the single action which required cocking the hammer before pulling the trigger. The pistol was very small, light and fit her small hands perfectly.

Sylvia asked, "can such a small pistol stop an aggressive man trying to kill me?"

"That small pistol shoots the same bullets that I have in my Colt and even in my 1873 rifle. It will stop a man better that a 10- pound sledge hammer."

Sylvia started shooting at a plank the width of a man set 6 yards away and missed all five shots. Max said, "relax, the gun will not hurt you, the man will. Use both hands to stop the shaking. This time she hit the plank all five times. Repeating the exercise, she eventually started hitting in a small circle. Eventually, she started shooting single hand. When she was managing this, he had her draw from a belt holster and fire with one hand. The last maneuver was to move the plank at 12 yards—the furthest distance for accurate self-defense.

Max spoke up, "that's enough hands on for today. Now come the do's and don'ts. This gun is for your defense and it must be worn on your body. When you need it is not the time to get it from the cabinet. If you are in the greenhouse and I'm not here, wear it. This is a gun for your defense. When you draw it from your holster, you have already decided that your life is in danger and you are drawing it to kill the aggressor. Shoot to kill, that will be your only chance to live. I will also recommend that if you shoot once, shoot again to guarantee the killer will fall. That is called a double tap and don't aim. Point and shoot your pistol at the center of the man's chest—called center mass.

"Killing a human being is horrendous, how do I explain my action to the law?"

"Always, always, always use and say repeatedly this same line. 'I feared for my life and knew this man was going to kill me. So, I shot him in self-defense.'"

"So, I answer any misleading questions with

the same line, and I don't volunteer any more information?"

"Yes, unless you have me or an attorney present who can guide you."

"By the way, what is this other holster for?"

"That's a shoulder holster that men wear under a vest. I forgot that it won't work for you, so stay with your belt holster."

"Why wouldn't it work for me?"

"Because your left breast is in the way"

"Now, Max Adams, you know I'm not that well-endowed."

"Well, we don't want to crush the little you have, heh?"

Sylvia smacked her hat on top of Max's chest and Max tried to get away. Before their antics were done, they were both in a passionate embrace.

Eventually, Max returned to the sheriff's office where he slept in the back room in return for being a resident deputy that allowed Wes to go back to the boarding house with Meg.

Meanwhile, at a ranch seventy miles south into Mexico, the Marquis Guerra called his segundo, Carlos Lopez, to the office. "Yes Patron, what is your wish?"

"Remember the Adams girl at the wedding a week ago?"

"Certainly, Patron."

"After much consideration, bring her to me. I want her broken-in by the time she arrives. Use whatever method you wish to make her subservient and receptive of my sexual needs. I am certain she already knows man which might make it easier on you. I have decided that I will make her give me an heir. A mixed blood heir that will bring my dynasty into the next century and intertwine with the Americans. This will be the gift to my ancestral line and will become my legacy."

"It will be done. I will take my best three men and set up a false trail to Laredo."

For the next three days, they worked side by side and by the third day, they had all the glass tubes seeded and watered. During those days, to fill time while working, Max started asking Sylvia about the business of growing and marketing vegetables.

"So, talk to me about this business of growing and marketing vegetables."

"Well, first, we grow six of the seven categories of vegetables:

1. Leafy green—lettuce and spinach.
2. Cruciferous—cabbage, cauliflower, brussels sprout, and broccoli.
3. Marrow—pumpkin, squash, cucumber, and tomatoes.
4. Root—potatoes, yams, carrots, beets and turnips.
5. Allium—onion, garlic, and shallots.
6. Pod—Beans, peas and string beans.
7. Plant Stem—celery and asparagus. This is the group we don't grow."

"Ok, that's a good start. Now, let's get into specifics. What are your best sellers?"

"Since we live on the border, the Mexican culture has a big influence on our market. So, our best sellers are Tomatoes, onions and peppers, especially the jalapeno pepper—the major ingredients in Mexican foods. Conversely, the major sellers for Americans is beans, potatoes, carrots, turnip and onions—the major ingredients in the American beef stew."

"What about fruits?

"We don't have fruit trees for grapefruits and oranges. These are already in the area and because it takes so long for a new tree to bear fruit, we decided not to plant them. Instead we plant a continuous ground crop of two fruits—watermelon, and cantaloupe."

"I thought tomatoes were a fruit."

"Only if you live back east. It can be either. In Texas we call it a vegetable—especially since we are a vegetable grower."

"Since we just finished seeding the winter transplants. What are the spring and summer transplants?"

"We start plants in the greenhouse that don't germinate well in the open field, have a long growing season or need protection from cold weather. For example, we plant tomatoes in February. By March we plant cucumbers, head lettuce, pumpkins and the two types of squash—summer, and zucchinis. In early summer we plant winter squash which need to harden in the cooler weather."

"That pretty much covers all the plants you start and mature in the greenhouse. Let's talk about planting seeds outside."

"First, the ground is cultivated to a workable loam from repeated passing of the finish harrows. Then we fertilize with composted horse/cow or chicken manure—the types available in the area.

Depending on the vegetable's need, we apply manure from 10 to 30 pounds to the 100 sq. ft. Tomatoes need much nitrogen, so they need the thicker application."

"Why composted manure?"

"Because of the high urea content that can burn and damage young plants. Composting for one year minimizes this damage."

"How do you know what to add to the soil for special nutrients."

"We send a soil sample to the University. According to their report we add special nutrients. For example: Epsom salt for magnesium or hardwood ashes for phosphate, as well as other available commercial minerals."

"Now, you've already described the field planting of the potted transplants. What about the remainder of vegetables?"

"Row planting on non-raised ground is the standard for a large grower. The crops include, for example: leaf lettuce, swiss chard, carrots, beets, onions, bush beans, peas, and corn. The planting is done by the new horse-drawn planters that set the distance between each seed.

Since we have a year-round growing season, we are beginning to plant some of the greenhouse potted plants directly into the ground thru our newly designed two-seater planter. We also have a potato planter and harvester that has replaced manual planting and harvesting."

"So, you have mechanized planting as much as possible. What about field care of the crops?"

"Obviously, the old method of manually tilling and weeding a backyard garden is out of the question. We have hundreds of acres to manage. All our work is done by horse-drawn tillers and crow-wings that back fill or hill up the rows."

"How much water is needed to grow crops in this desert area?"

"The area gets an average of 20 inches of rain per year. Without irrigation, you have no crops. We irrigate by flooding a plot or individual rows. The irrigation canals are crucial in bringing water to the plants. As an average, plants in this hot sun need an inch of water each week. The more the planted acreage, the more windmill pumps you need. As of now, we have six windmill pumps and six corresponding holding ponds. We hope that this is the right ratio to water 100 acres this year, but time will tell."

"How do you preserve harvested crops."

"Obviously, we harvest what we hope to sell at the farmer's market each week. Yet there are crops that need to be harvested when ready and may need storage. We are planning to hire the Mexican force to dig a six-foot root cellar and cover it with an insulated roof. Some vegetables need to be harvested a bit before maturity while others are harvested post maturity. Both can be stored if maintained in a cool and dry space such as in the root cellar."

"That's a lot of knowledge, but I presume that knowing how to grow vegetables is not enough. You need a market to sell your crops. Where are you planning to sell your crops?"

"We have now developed two retail sites and one wholesale buyer. I will bring a display wagon to town each Friday and set up at the farmer's market. Brian goes east some eight miles with a loaded wagon of vegetables and heads to a settlement not yet named. Dad arranges for crates to be freighted to the ferry and shipped down river to our wholesaler in Brownsville. This wholesale buyer takes anything that did not sell for the week, plus anything else we want to send."

"What do you do with rotting or post mature plants?"

"We have a pig farmer pick them up weekly at a bargain price."

"Looking overall, what is the one vegetable that is a steady seller?"

"Beans, beans, and more beans. This is a very affordable food. The bulk of the sales are navy beans, but we sell black, pinto and kidney beans. Beans are served as the main dish, or in soups, stews and many Tex-Mex dishes. We keep a fresh crop by replanting every 21 days."

"To summarize, the five of you divide your days working in the greenhouse, field planting, tilling and hoeing crops, selling at the markets, irrigating, cultivating plots for the next planting, and cultivating more land for future growth."

"Yes, and the way you say it, I believe we'll be hiring workers soon, heh?"

Working together during the honeymooner's absence was a gratifying time. Not only did Max learn about olericulture, he got comfortable with the woman he was falling in love with. They talked continuously and never ran out of subject matter. Periodically there was some show of affection marked by a touch, hug and kiss. It was clear that they were bonding and falling in love.

Meanwhile, for the past two days, Sylvia and Max never realized that they were under surveillance. Hidden 400 yards away in a clump of trees, were four Mexicans watching them thru binoculars. The one consistent clue they found useful was the fact that the maiden came to the greenhouse several hours before her parents awoke, or the policeman arrived on the premises.

As Max was preparing to return to town for his night shift at the sheriff's office, Sylvia reminded him, that with the greenhouse work completed, tomorrow they would spend the day sitting behind a horse. One would disc harrow and the other finish harrow a plot being readied for irrigation and planting.

Without the extra sense of predicting the future, neither of them could foresee how the next weeks would shape their future lives, forever!

***

CHAPTER 9—The Rescue

The next morning, Sylvia was up a bit earlier to help her dad harness the gelding to the buckboard. Grant and Nellie were going to town for supplies and bringing the newlyweds back home.

After the Cassidys left, Sylvia went to the greenhouse with her mug of coffee, to do some watering till Max arrived. Sylvia had armed herself with her loaded Bulldog since she was alone. Sitting at her desk, she began daydreaming about her burgeoning relationship with Max. Being lost in thought, she did not notice the visitors entering the greenhouse. Suddenly, she felt a knife on her throat and was yanked to stand up. The Mexican voice said, "Senorita, do not resist and you will remain safe."

Sylvia reacted instantly. She drew her pistol and pointed it backwards at her assailant. As per practice, she fired a double tap and both shots emitted loud screams of pain as she felt a tap on her head, and all went black. Sylvia never realized that she had hit the intruder in the knee-cap on the first shot and in the foot on the second shot.

Her unconscious body was straddled and tied to a horse, as the four Mexicans headed east along the river to a prearranged rendezvous location.

Max got up late the next morning and had his breakfast at Kate's Diner. Shortly thereafter, he got his horse at Sammy's livery and headed out of town. Passing by Stevenson's Mercantile, he saw Grant and Nellie loading up supplies. He stopped to talk to them.

"Might as well stop at Emerson's Hardware, I ordered a tubing, adapter and stop-cock to replace the one I used up."

"Will do, and that new tubing is called 'rubber.'"

"Really, well we'll see you at the farm."

"We may be a bit late, we're having breakfast with Brian and Jenna. They're supposed to be returning to the farm today."

Riding from town, Max would let his horse have his head. He would slow gallop the entire four miles and would cover the distance in twenty minutes. Arriving at the farm, Max would bring his horse to the barn, unsaddle, rub down and feed him. Today Max was a bit surprised to see the two teams of work horses still in their stalls.

He expected them to be already harnessed and ready to go.

Walking to the kitchen's backdoor, no one was in the house. He then headed for the greenhouse. As he walked in, he spotted Sylvia's Bulldog pistol on the ground next to her desk. Next to the pistol was a large pool of dried blood. Following the blood trail outside, it stopped where there were several hoofed prints of at least five horses. Examining the hoof sizes, it was clear that all five horses were small horses that were common among Mexicans and showed signs of unique forging again common among Mexican blacksmiths. Max knew Sylvia had been kidnapped and recognized he had to warn the sheriff in case this was part of a master kidnapping ring in the area.

Max raced back to town and alerted Wes who would warn all the homesteaders for the ten miles east of town. He then had three stops. He went to Sammy's livery and asked for him to saddle his packhorse. Then he stopped at Stevenson's Mercantile and asked Elmer to immediately get his usual list of supplies ready. His last stop was Kate's Diner and informed Sylvia's family of her kidnapping. When Grant and Brian offered to go after the kidnappers, Max made it clear that he could do this best if he was alone. Knowing Max's reputation, they quickly backed down and let Max leave. Max picked up his packhorse, his trail equipment, food, and his long-range rifle.

Returning to the Cassidy homestead, he picked up the five-horse trail. He computed that they had a four-hour head start or approximately a twenty-mile lead, depending how fast Sylvia could travel.

Meanwhile, Sylvia had awakened shortly after beginning to ride off. She screamed until they untied her and let her sit in the horse's saddle with her manacled hands tied to the saddle horn. Carlos led the Mexicans and Sylvia to the rendezvous point. They rode into the shallow Rio Grande river and met with five Gringoes who were also waiting for Carlos in the river. Without any greeting, Carlos asked if the Gringoes had traveled only in the river from the east. When answered, "we did as agreed. We traveled at least a mile from the east and only in the water, sometimes we had to swim the horses, but we managed." "Very good, here is your $500. Now get on land and pretend to travel back to Laredo, but a mile from here split up and go five different ways—and hurry so you are not captured by the

American lawman." As the Gringoes headed for shore, Carlos and his caravan rode west along the Mexican side of the river and turned south many miles later when the water required the horses to swim. Once on land, they had seventy miles to travel, and many days to subdue this aggressive and combative Gringo woman.

Max was riding at a slow trot and tracking to match his speed. It was clear that the kidnappers were not trying to hide their tracks. It wasn't clear to Max why they were heading west. At the beginning, he thought they were going to start kidnapping along the eastern settlements and homesteads. However, it was clear that the tracks stayed away from all those locations. Irrelevant that the outlaws were heading west to Laredo, they were Mexicans and would eventually turn south to Mexico.

Max stayed on the trail and by mid afternoon the tracks rode right in the river. Max assumed it was to water the horses before turning to the south. To his surprise, the tracks of five horses went to the west again, on the American side of the river. Happy to have quickly found the tracks, he hurriedly got on the trail again. He aggressively followed the tracks till darkness was approaching. Suddenly at a watering hole, the tracks split up into five different tracks. Max got off his horse and more carefully examined the tracks. Max slapped his forehead and said, "what an idiot, I let my emotions control my actions. These are not Mexican horse tracks, they are the large hoofs of American horses. They made a switch and now I am a full day behind. By morning I will return to the river and pickup the Mexican horse tracks."

Max even considered returning to the river during full darkness without a moon. He knew that this was dangerous for the horses to fall and break a leg, which would make him even more behind. Wisely, he unsaddled the horses and set up camp. He started a small fire to cook his dinner of beans, bacon, biscuits and coffee. After a good night's sleep, he would go back in the morning and start over.

Meanwhile, some twenty miles south of the border, the caravan had stopped for the night. Sylvia asked, "where can I use the bushes?" Carlos answered, "here, on the ground in front of us."

"I demand some privacy, we are not animals."

Before another word was said, a whip snap

was heard and landed on Sylvia's rear end. Sylvia almost collapsed but did not scream. Carlos repeated, "you don't demand, you ask. When we order you, you respond without backtalk! Now squat and relieve yourself."

"Thank you, I will not, you ass hole."

Carlos was furious, took the whip and landed two powerful hits on Sylvia's chest, tearing her blouse and chemise and exposing her breasts. Sylvia saw stars and collapsed to the ground, while relieving herself in the process. When she woke up, she was naked and staked spread eagle to the ground. The Mexicans were having dinner and offered nothing to Sylvia. She spent the chilly night without cover. In the morning, Carlos threw her pants and shirt, and told her to dress for the days ride. Once her bindings were cut, Sylvia never spoke but took the time to relieve herself on the spot before dressing.

Leaving camp, Sylvia was again tied to the saddle horn. Once on the trail, Carlos sent two of his men off to the west, and the remainder of the caravan continued south. Sylvia thought, *"he is sending two men off on a decoy to ambush Max. Max will likely think that I am on this trail and will ride into a trap.*

Max broke camp in predawn and was heading back to the river as soon as daybreak. Arriving at the river, he had to walk the shoreline on both sides to find an exit onto land. It took almost a half day to finally see where the five horses had exited the river, and they were the hoof marks of small Mexican horses. Back on the trail, but now he had to be wary of an ambush at any turn or behind any cover. He had to slow down and follow his gut feeling.

Max thought, "*in this terrain, an ambush would come from several locations: boulders especially some high ones, clumps of trees, a rise in the trail providing high ground, gullies and cliffs. His only defense was a premonition/gut feeling or warning from his horse. Most ambushes came from 100 yards or less. The one physical landmark of an ambush ahead was the tracks. When a band of outlaws stop riding, their horses' pace about and leave extra tracks. The one absolute proof of an ambush is when the outlaws resume riding, but one track goes off to the side.*

Sometimes, the gang brings the shooter's horse with them to hide it down-trail. That requires a very alert tracker to notice the light hoof marks of a rider-less horse.

Max was pushing his horse. He knew he was

way behind the kidnappers. In his mind, the recovery rate of kidnapped victims goes drastically down by each passing day. This was his second day and he knew he needed to get close on their heels.

Meanwhile some ten miles away, the caravan was stopped. Carlos spoke to two of his men, "I want you two to ride west about five miles and then start looking for a good spot to set up an ambush. Once you drygulch our tail, then return to the Patron's ranch with the Gringoe's horse. Make sure the tail is dead. If no one arrives within two days, come home."

Pushing on, Max saw a steady pattern to the tracks for at least ten miles. Suddenly, he rode to a patch of ground that had evidence of some milling around. He then identified two tracks veering off to the west and the other four continuing south. *How to choose. Did the lead kidnapper take the hostage and headed west to his destination? Or did the leader send two of his men as decoys with or without an ambush.* He decided to go west after the double track. If it was Sylvia's trail, he would rescue her soon. If it was the outlaw's trail, he would capture at least one alive and make him talk. Max needed to know the kidnapper's destination in case he lost their trail.

Max resumed tracking. This trail was full of good ambush sites. Max knew it was impossible to go around each one since it would take weeks to move along. He decided he had to presume the Mexican men were poor shots and had to risk a fake fatal wound. So, he moved along at a fast walk and sometimes a slow trot. He had to risk his life in order to save Sylvia's.

Meanwhile, Carlos was stopping some fifteen miles further south. Once off her horse, she asked Carlos if she could go to the bushes. Sylvia thought, "*it's better to ask permission for an insignificant issue than being whipped to a pulp. It's a matter of survival, not submission, until Max arrives.*

As the Mexicans ate dinner, all Sylvia got was water. After dinner, Carlos came up to Sylvia and said, "you have been chosen to be my Patron's mistress and to give him an heir. If you agree to this commitment, you will get food, water and will no longer be tied to your horse. If not, we will stay in this camp, beat you and sexually assault you into submission. Tell me your choice, now."

Sylvia did not pause, "I know who your 'Patron' is. He's that so-called nobleman by the name of Guerra who was at my brother's wedding. Well, it will be a cold day in hell when I submit to that fake human being living in his ancestral past. I will never submit to you or your Patron's demands."

Carlos responded by throwing back his bull whip and twice striking her in the chest and abdomen. Sylvia fell to her knees, in excruciating pain, but more determined to resist his demands. Carlos stepped up to her and said, "you, stupid woman, you'll learn the hard way." He then swung his foot and hit her in the face. Sylvia collapsed and passed out. She awoke to find herself again tied in four points/spread eagle on the ground. When she lifted her head to look at the whip marks, she again noticed that she was naked in preparation of the chilly night. She wondered if she had been raped when unconscious but could not examine herself while bound to the ground.

Max was still moving up the trail. The two Mexican men had been drinking heavily while waiting for a visitor. Carlos had made two mistakes when he sent these two incompetents on a mission: he let them have their tequila and never realized they only had one rifle.

The men spoke, "I think we have waited long enough, tomorrow we close camp and leave." "I agree, besides, if a Gringo shows up today, who will shoot him with the rifle, we are both drunk." "Since I have poor vision naturally, you will have to do the shooting, heh."

Not realizing anything different, Max was approaching the ambush site. Always ready to react, a shot came from somewhere in the trees. Max felt the hot lead strafe his left biceps and naturally faked a major hit. He quickly lifted himself on his stirrups and threw his body off the horse—lying still on the ground and playing dead.

Max could hear the Mexicans talking, "hey Pedro, you clearly had a major hit, let's walk down to make sure he is dead."

As the Mexicans were walking toward him, Max waited till they were ten yards away. When Pedro pointed his rifle at Max, Max pulled his colt and shot him in the head. The other Mexican was so shocked that he lifted his hands in the air and said, "don't shoot senor, I give up."

Max sat the man down and tied him to a tree,

went to get something in his saddlebags and said, "I need to know where you are taking the prisoner and who ordered the kidnapping."

"Senor, I cannot say, for I will be executed for revealing such information."

"Mister, you will tell me sooner or later. Since I want to know now, I will torture you. Instead, tell me what I need to know, and I will l let you live without torture—that's your best deal.

The Mexican responded, "I do not believe you will torture me, I happen to know you are a lawman and we all know lawmen do not do this."

Max's face stiffened and the Mexican placed his hands on the ground to push his body back. Max said, "today, I am a US citizen out to rescue the woman I will marry. You are the enemy, as he swung the awl in his right hand and implanted it in the Mexican's left hand. The Mexican howled in total surprise. To make it worse, Max started bending the awl in multiple direction, each move eliciting another loud scream.

Pulling the awl out, he asked, "are you ready to talk?"

With the Mexican shaking his head in the negative, Max pushed his lower jaw down and shoved the awl deep in a black/rotten molar.

The result took Max by surprise. The Mexican's body instantly stiffened, follow by his sphincters relaxing. As Max was giggling the awl around, the Mexican was screaming to high heavens as he soiled his britches.

Max pulled the awl out, and with the stench, he hoped the Mexican would answer his demand. When asked, the Mexican refused again. Max didn't even hesitate, he poked another tooth and this time the Mexican passed out. Once awakened, Max said, "I saw another nine rotten teeth and we can continue this affront."

"To avoid execution, I will have to disappear deep in the western center of the country. I will need three things: a canteen full of water, my knife, and my shotgun with buckshot ammo for self-defense from bandits, and the ability to hunt game for my survival."

"Done, I will even include $50 in cash to make your trip easier."

"The segundo, Carlos Lopez, is bringing your maiden to Marquis Juan Guerra, some forty miles from here."

"For what purpose?"

"To become the Patron's mistress and mother of his heirs."

Max allowed the Mexican to go to the stream to clean himself and his britches. When he returned, Max gave him the canteen, the cash and his unloaded shotgun. Max would leave the box of buckshot shotgun shells on a blow-down pine tree some two hundred yards on the back trail. Max left with both horses on a trail rope behind his packhorse and with all firearms in the panniers. Five miles later he was again on the trail going south. The tracks had dried but at a slower riding rate, caused by three horses on trail ropes, he could still follow along.

A few miles later, Max came upon a surprise—a small town. He went straight to the one livery and offered to sell the two Mexican saddled horses with two pistols and one rifle. The livery man was interested but admitted he had limited funds. When Max pretended to leave, the livery man said, "wait, I can offer you 500 pesos which is about $100 in US funds. Max said, "I'll accept 400 pesos as adequate payment from an honest man."

Max then went to the only mercantile in town. He walked in and asked the owner if three Mexicans and an American woman had come to buy supplies—as he passed a $20 double eagle on the table. The clerk said in good English, "Yes, two days ago. They bought enough supplies for a week and when they left, they headed south."

Meanwhile in Carlos's camp, Sylvia froze all night as well as writhing in pain from the deep tracks and welts on her chest and abdomen. After the Mexicans had their breakfast, Carlos came over to cut her ground bindings and offered her all the water she needed to prevent dehydration. He then asked, "have you changed your mind?"

"Never in a million years," as she spat in his face.

Carlos was again furious. He ordered his men to stand the prisoner up and tie her hands high to two trees. Gloria stood there totally naked as Carlos whipped her repeatedly. His aim was Gloria's breasts and private area—the two most sensitive areas on her body. Gloria screamed but didn't beg him to stop. It was Carlos's men who suggested that the woman had had enough and encouraged him to stop whipping her. Carlos put his whip down and walked away leaving Sylvia to bleed from several of her deep gouges. Sylvia was near unconsciousness, her body was limp, her head bent over, and lifeless. The two Mexicans cut her wrist bindings and gently laid her on her back on the ground.

Max was making good time and to his surprise, he started smelling campfire smoke. He did not expect to find their camp so soon. It only meant that they had not been moving for some time. It also meant that Sylvia was being physically or sexually tortured into submission. Despite these terrible possibilities, justice and rescue was at hand.

Max tied his horses to a branch, took his scoped 1876 rifle and started walking toward the smoke smell. At three hundred yards, he set up a solid rifle rest and scoped the camp. Gloria was lying naked on the ground and the Mexicans were sitting by the campfire drinking their tequila. Max could not see an easy camp access since the open land would make his access impossible during daylight. Yet, he would continue to observe the goings on to make sure Sylvia was not in current danger and planned a nighttime attack—little did he know the torture she had already endured.

In camp, Carlos's men were eager to ravage the prisoner. They addressed their leader, "the maiden is not budging despite the torture. Could it be that she has never had a man and is a virgin? If that's the case, knowing she is still chaste may be the reason she is so resistant. If we were to have her, it could change her attitude in the face of more torture."

"Yes, you may be right. She may be saving herself for her policeman lover, and while still intact she will continue to resist. This issue was mentioned by our Patron. He hinted that we were allowed to use whatever means to make her submissive. Very well, I will take her first and then you will both have your turn. Let us enjoy our tequila until she awakens."

Max was still watching the Mexicans drinking. Suddenly, they all got up and walked to Sylvia. They tied her again in spread eagle fashion and threw cold water in her face to awaken. In his scope he could see that Gloria awoke with a startled look as she realized she was again tied spread eagle. The deciding factor was when the Mexican, he recognized as the segundo, stood between Sylvia's legs and dropped his trousers and gun belt. Max knew he had to act now.

Max had to decide who to shoot first, the segundo or the two bystanders. Without a second thought, Max shot the two bystanders as he saw the segundo move to Sylvia head and applied a knife to her neck. Max put his rifle down and ran into the camp. As he arrived, the segundo was still holding a knife to Sylvia's neck and said, "let me dress and leave and I will not harm your woman. After all, she is what you want unharmed, heh?"

"I cannot allow that. I want her alive and you dead." Max drew his Colt and fired. As expected, a bullet to his private sac caused so much pain that, by reflex, he moved his right hand holding the knife to his crotch in an attempt to heal and protect himself. He dropped the knife and Max stepped up. He grabbed the segundo by his shirt lapel and punched him in the face three times. He then took the segundo's whip and smacked him several times. Finally, he tied the whip around his neck and swung the other end over a limb. He pulled and hung the animal to a slow death. As he was choking to death, he told him, "I don't risk my life or the life of my woman to save an animal outlaw. I will always kill, in the future, to save our lives."

Sylvia was watching Max and the entire hanging. She was so filled with anger and hate that she never tried to stop Max. After Carlos died, Max cut the whip and let his body fall to the ground. He stepped to Sylvia and said, "I promise that I will protect you forever, so help me God. Your ordeal is over, and I will do my best to keep you at peace. I love you so much and would you marry me?"

"In my heart, you're already my husband. Yes, I want to be your wife and I will love you forever." Sylvia started crying, out of joy, despite her abused and macerated body.

***

CHAPTER 10—Healing and Restitution

Max leaned over Sylvia and said, "the first thing we need to do is to treat your many cuts and welts. We have no medicines, but we need to shrink the welts and clean the cuts. I recommend I immerse you in the cool stream which will accomplish both needs."

"Sounds like the answer. I'm so weak, though, that I can't even sit up and certainly cannot walk."

"Not a problem. I will carry you." Max stands up and takes his shirt off, gun belt and britches. Standing nude, Sylvia asked what he was up to.

I'm going to put you in a deep hole to be totally immersed. That means I have to be with you since I suspect a land lover will not know how to swim, right?"

"Yes."

"Well, I don't have a change of clothes and I want my clothes to stay dry. So, since we're engaged, forget modesty and let's go."

Max gently picked her up and carried her to the stream. Walking in, Sylvia gasped and said, "you said the cool stream, this is frigging ice cold. Max started to laugh to hide his own shock. Eventually their bodies adjusted to the water temperature. "You were right, my skin is numb, and the pain is subsiding."

"Now, let me rub your open cuts and sores to clean them out."

Max was busy gently rubbing her skin when Gloria said, "some of the parts you're rubbing are rather personal and sensitive. Is this going to get you in distress again?"

"Normally, just the thought of it would get me in distress. In this ice pack, everything has shriveled into hibernation. Hopefully, a temporary situation!"

After a long soak, Max carried her back to camp and had her stand as he laid out a bedroll next to the fire pit. Checking her backside, he found her bottom had a few old marks. He got Sylvia to lay on her back on the bedroll. He then went to get a bottle of tequila and sterilized all the open wounds. Sylvia gritted her teeth but tolerated the burning from the alcohol. As he finished, he said, "let your skin dry as I have other duties to get to." "Sylvia added, "such as?"

"I need to drag these bodies away from camp

before predators come visiting, and we need to start a fire and prepare you some food.

"Before all that, I need you to do something for me."

"I can't sit up, but I need to know if they raped me when I was unconscious. I need for you to examine me and let me know the truth."

"Uh, I'm no doctor and……..!"

"Oh, bull ticky, you've been with women and I'm sure you can tell me if I'm still intact. So, please."

There were no more discussions and Max carefully proceeded with the personal task. Without floundering over Sylvia's anatomy, he quickly said, "without any doubt, you are very much intact. Now stop worrying since it would not have made a difference if you'd not been. I love everything about you, your soul, mind, personality, beautiful looks, and being with you is the joy in my life. Now, let's get to work."

First, Max dragged the three bodies some three hundred yards downwind. He saved some clothing that might fit Sylvia. When he returned to camp, he looked in the three saddlebags and found a few pesos but also found $200 US and pocketed the funds. He also found an antiseptic ointment in one bag and decided to apply it to Sylvia's worse cuts and abrasions. As he was applying the ointment, he again reminded Sylvia that she was an unbelievable mole, hiding such a beautiful body. Sylvia merely laughed, a laugh that said "gotcha."

After preparing a meal of beef stew, he helped spoon feed Sylvia. The last thing on tonight's agenda was covering her body. He tried to lay a blanket on her, but the pain was unbearable. Instead, he went in the woods and selected a half dozen 3-4-foot saplings that were flexible. Over her body he bent the saplings to form a hoop and then covered the hoops with the wool blankets. The blanket ends covered her shoulders and neck as well as her legs. Being placed next to the fire, Sylvia was looking forward to a comfortable night's sleep.

Once the morning temperature warmed up, Max took down the hooped tent. Sylvia was able to sit and then stand as she groaned thru the drawing and stretching of the whip burns. She walked around and when she got tired, would sit on a large round piece of unsplit firewood. After a boosting breakfast of bacon and fried potatoes, Max suggested that Sylvia might consider some clothes. She started with a loose shirt but could not tolerate the burning sensation.

She then said, "I can't stand this shirt, and won't even consider britches. Guess you'll need to tolerate your fiancé walking around nude all day. Other than that, where do we go from here?"

"Ok, here me out. We stay in this camp all week or longer if needed. We are not traveling till you are healed and can ride. We have plenty of food, water and the horses have plenty of forage. I will build a tent, with the several tarps we have, in case it starts raining. Then and only then do we head home or go south to visit the honorable Juan Guerra."

Sylvia's eyes lit up. "I have been thinking that this man needs to be made aware that we know what he did. He needs to be convinced that a repeat performance would lead to serious results."

"Realistically, we need to put the fear of God into him and some physical punishment is in order. If it works, we will be free of him forever. If it fails, we will have to deal with the assassins he sends us. In this case, we'll need to return to Mexico to kill him."

"I agree, it is the nature of the beast, and we have to deal with it."

The week turned out to be a special time for a couple in love, who had made a commitment to each other. Once Sylvia was able to wear clothes, she wore a loose wool shirt and soft Mexican cotton pants. At night time, they enjoyed sleeping together in the tarp tent. The love making progressed slowly because of Sylvia's lesions. Yet, it had eventually extended in the realm of enjoying mutual pleasures. Consummation of their engagement would have to wait a better time.

Max went hunting and came back with a medium size deer. Their first meal was liver and thereafter it was venison stew or steaks. With the other staples and coffee, they ate very well all week. Fortunately, the Mexicans had several cans of potatoes, carrots, onions and tomatoes which would supplement the steaks or stews. They had plenty of bacon, canned beans, fresh fried potatoes, and biscuits for breakfast. Anticipating getting back on the trail, they started to separate and save trail foods. Max had built a make shift smoker and had smoked the venison to help preserve the meat for the anticipated trip.

As the time arrived, before they broke camp,

Max handed Sylvia her Webley Bulldog pistol. "Wear it until we get home. Whether it's for self-defense against humans, animals or rattlesnakes, it's only available if you're wearing it."

They now had five saddled horses and one packhorse. Sylvia was allowed to ride freely on her horse while Max trailed the other four horses. It was slow going and as soon as they got to a small town, they were fortunate to sell the three Mexican horses and tack for $100 US. Max kept the Mexican's guns, since they were all US made Winchesters and Colts.

They traveled at a comfortable speed till nightfall. Setting up camp and cooking dinner was Sylvia's job, as Max took care of the horses and set up a two-man tent that they had purchased at the last Mexican town. After dinner, Max said, "we should talk about two crucial issues!"

"And they are?"

"How we are going to deal with that Mexican dirt bag, and what will be my function as your husband on your vegetable farm?"

"Let's deal with the Marquis, first."

"I think we should arrive at the ranch in mid-morning when the hands are working the herd. We will instruct the housekeeper that we are a delegation from an American hay producer and need to speak to the Marquis about signing a contract."

"Well that gets us in without gunfire. Then what?"

"Then I will deal out some justice and leave a mark on his face. He will be marked for life as a lowlife and a patron that sent his men to their death. In addition, he will know that any repeated attempt on your life will mean his death."

"What about me, I need to get some restitution."

Max hands her a six-inch tool. Sylvia asks, "what is this and what do I do with it?"

"This is a Marlin nail—a Cowboy tool. It has one pointed end and a rounded end into a loop. The loop fits in your palm to push the point into leather to make holes or to unbraid leather strips."

"I see, now what do I do with it?"

"When we get into the Marquis's office, he will have the shock of his life when he see's you. To get his attention, plant this nail in any part of his face, hands or arms—that way he'll know we are not on a business mission for you dad. I will then take over my part."

"That was straight forward. I approve, I didn't

want to kill him either, to mark him for what he is, is certainly the best justice."

"Now when we get home, I will abandon my bounty hunting days. It is such a dangerous profession, that I would never take on a wife and children with such a burden. I could become a deputy sheriff or even a Texas Ranger, but that defeats the goal of spending my life with you. So how do I fit in as the boss's husband."

"Max, you are a leader and eventually you will be the farm foreman and later the manager/ owner. Yet, as a greenhorn, you must start at the bottom. Dad will certainly take you under his wings. He will teach you how to drive horses to plow, harrow, spread manure, seed and build irrigation ditches. Then he will show you how to till the planted rows. We will all participate in the harvest and even send you with Brian to learn the marketing business."

"This looks like a sound plan, and I'm willing to learn. How long will this apprentice program last?"

"One full year, to go thru several complete planting cycles, and to cover one year of business. In view of the fact that we are planning to add Mexican or American workers, you need to show you have mastered every business division—from handling manure to collecting money, heh!"

"I can do it and looking forward to the challenge. Plus, I need some of your Olericulture books as I learn each division. This will give me an edge for the future."

"Now, a subject that I'm leery to broach. How much gunwork will you be involved with?"

"Barring some catastrophe that Wes or Sheriff McFarlane cannot handle, I only plan to defend and protect us and our families from those who wish us harm."

"Such as?"

"From my bounty hunter years, there may be some friends or family members that want revenge for killing or bringing their outlaws to the gallows. Marquis Guerra may send assassins after us, the human traffickers may try to abduct you, Jenna or our mom's. Even robbers may try to steal our money from the market sales. And there are always psychopaths that cause depredations for no reason. Then on the other hand, maybe none of this will happen."

"Well, it's not anything we can plan for. However, Brian and I do not leave the market with cash. Before heading home, we make a deposit in the local bank where we have an account."

"It's not a matter of planning, it's a matter of being ready. Every worker has to be somewhat proficient with a rifle that must be available in the fields, on their implements or in the barns. You need to wear your Bulldog for at least a year, morning to bedtime. I will always have my Colt 45 on my belt or attached to the implement I'm working with. Respond to rumors, reliable or questionable, by going on high alert."

That brought them close to midnight according to Max's pocket watch. They then retired to their mini-tent for some private affectionate display of their passion and fell asleep in each-other's arms. During the night, Sylvia needed to go to the bushes. Realizing Max was sound asleep, she belted her Bulldog to her hip. While doing her business, a large mangy and salivating coyote appeared four feet away. In the moonlight, she pulled her pistol, aimed, and easily dispatched the "mad" animal.

The gunshot brought Max to instant awareness, when he saw that Sylvia was not in the tent, he jumped to his knees, grabbed his pistol and dove for the tent door. Max didn't realize, till it was too late, and dove into the rear of the tent thinking in was the exit door side. The tent collapsed on top of him, and by the time he found his way out, Sylvia was standing over him, laughing out loud.

Max was quick to rattle off, where did you go, who fired that gun, and a few other useless questions. Sylvia described the entire trappings and added that she didn't want to awaken him to escort her to the bushes.

Max said nothing, holstered his pistol and walked over to the coyote. "This animal likely has the disease called 'rabies' or 'mad dog.' Had you been bitten, you would have had a fatal illness after going mad. That's why, in the wild, you must always be prepared—having a gun in your hand evens up the odds."

"With the tent totally in shambles, they decided to roll it up with the bedrolls, and prepare coffee and breakfast. Max got the horses saddled and Sylvia cleaned the dishes and closed camp. The were then off on their last leg of their journey.

Arriving at the Guerra hacienda, Max tied the packhorse to a branch and slowly rode into the yard. They knocked and a housekeeper came to the door. Sylvia introduced herself as a representative of the Adams hay company. She wished an interview to sign a contract for the next year. The housekeeper said, "wait here, I will introduce you. You only have thirty minutes since the Marquis has an engagement every Tuesday at 10AM."

Entering the office, Guerra was reading and never looked up. He spoke without looking at his visitors and said, "this is highly unusual," as he looked up. With his mouth open he stood up and placed the palm of both hands on his desk and said, "what is the meaning of this intrusion?"

"As per your request, I am here." Sylvia lifted the Marlin nail and with both hands impaled it thru the Marquis' left hand and solidly planted into the desk-top. Guerra squealed and screamed as he tried to remove the nail. Sylvia said, "that's for abducting, beating and ordering your men to defile me—you piece of crap."

Max then stepped up, grabbed his free hand and nonchalantly grabbed the index and middle finger and hyperextended them thru several snapping sounds till both fingers touched the back of his hands. Guerra had a look of total disbelief and continued moaning. Max then said, "now, I'm going to mark you for the animal you are. He grabbed his shirt collar and with a leathered glove hand, pummeled him three times in the mouth till all the front teeth went flying. At the end, he took his knife and snipped off a half inch of the Marquis' nose. The Marquis was yelling for help as he tried to stop the gushing blood from his amputated nose tip. By using his thumb and ring finger, he wasn't very successful in even slowing the bleeding.

As they were leaving, Max added, "Carlos and most of his men are dead. This will be your fate if you send assassins after us. Now with your puckered-up nose and toothless mouth, you will look like a pig, and that will reflect on you forever—an appropriate appearance for a psychopathic and filthy rutting animal."

As they exited the office, the ghostly looking housekeeper was standing with her hands to her mouth. Sylvia said, "no rush, he's not going anywhere." By the time they were on the porch, the housekeeper came running out and screaming for the cook to come help the patron. With Max and Sylvia on their horse, the cook arrived with the housekeeper at his side. Max yelled out, "better go back to the barn and get a crowbar.

Whatever you do, don't laugh at Mr. Piggy, or your going to be a dead cook, real quick!"

Heading back home, they traveled at a good speed till dark and two hours beyond under moonlight. They had covered thirty miles and were exhausted. They decided to stop and get some rest. They would be in the safety of their home by tomorrow. Sylvia asked what the chances were that Guerra would send a killing party onto their trail today.

Max answered, "despite our warning, it's 100% certain that we will have visitors tonight. Consequently, we'll set up a safe camp."

Sylvia didn't know how to set up a safe camp and just watched Max at work. Max started a good campfire for cooking and Sylvia gathered enough firewood to keep the fire going all night. The three horses were tethered far away to avoid catching a bullet. Max then set out a rope six inches off the ground, circled the entire camp, and tied several cowbells to the ropes. He then set up the tent next to the fire, but moved their bedroll some 30 yards away, hidden behind bushes.

At bedtime, Max gave Sylvia a double barrel shotgun with six OO Buckshot shells, as Max also loaded his sawed-off shotgun. Max said, "when it comes time to shoot, I will shoot both barrels at the men on the left, and you shoot the ones on the right, and shoot twice like I will do. Don't hesitate, these men will be here to kill us, and we'll only get one chance. If you hesitate, the gun smoke will impair your vision. So, shoot as soon as I do. Ok?"

"You can rely on me, I'll do my part."

"After the way you planted that Marlin nail, I know you will."

Sound asleep, a cowbell exploded as someone tripped and fell to his knees. Several men responded and started shooting at the tent. Max yelled out. "Stop or you're dead." The visitors turned their weapons toward the sound, but Max immediately fired. By his second shot, Sylvia was on his tail and fired her first shot. After the four shots from the shotguns, there was no visibility. As the smoke cleared, Sylvia reloaded her shotgun as Max drew his pistol. Yet there was no need, since all five Mexican killers were dead.

Being close to predawn, they decided to start breakfast and prepare to close camp. The dead men's pockets were searched and revealed 2,500 pesos. Max figured, a new tent would cost that much so he pocketed the money. Again, the firearms were good American quality, and he would keep them to arm his own workers in the Valley. The bodies were left to the predators, and the caravan again trailed five saddled Mexican horses.

Arriving in town, they visited Sammy's Livery. Sammy checked the horses and the saddles. He finally said, "this is a valuable group of horses. They are young and sure-footed horses. They would appeal to American or Mexican ranchers. Let's try something different. Let's see what I can get for them and I will charge you 15% as my commission.

Before going home, they stopped at the jeweler's shop to buy their wedding rings, made an arrangement with their minister, filled out the marriage license and arranged for Kate's diner to cater a meal at the parish hall.

As they made their way to the Cassidy homestead, each was woolgathering about their future. Both were thinking of their wedding. Max was thinking of his apprentice year and how he would protect himself and others from outlaws seeking revenge. Sylvia looked at her year as one with so many new things. A husband, possibly a first child, managing a new business. The light at the end of the tunnel was making her husband an equal in managing the business by the end of the year.

***

BOOK FOUR

THE DREAM

CHAPTER 11—A New Day

With the marriage license in hand, Max said, "the courthouse is right here. Have you considered getting married right now and spend our wedding night at the Winslow Hotel? Tomorrow, we would arrive unexpected at home, not only alive, but a married couple."

"You know I would like that, but that's not going to happen. Our parents haven't had a moment's peace since my abduction, and to show up married would deny my parents the joy and right to put on a wedding for their only daughter."

Jokingly, Max added, "so, are we being respectful or considerate?"

"Neither, it's just right, and when it feels right, it usually is!"

"Um…seems like I've already used that line, before we uh……?"

Arriving home at lunch time, all four family members were in the kitchen, Sylvia and Max quietly hitched their horses to the hitching rail and sneaked in the house. Max bellowed out, "anybody home?"

Nellie was first to respond, as she turned in the doorway to see her daughter standing proud in the parlor. The reunion was full of hugs, kisses and tears of joy. It was Grant that finally spoke. We were so worried, it was beyond belief. Not knowing is always man's downfall and this was no exception. Without telegraph service, no one had any news. Even Sheriff Silvers couldn't get any news by having Gary Sweeney relay a telegram to Mexico City or Monterrey police departments. But now, that's in the past and you're finally home."

Brian said, "tell us about your ordeal."

Max went thru the story rather quickly but went into detail about their encounter with the Marquis. When Grant realized, who was to blame for Sylvia's ordeal, he knew Max's dad would feel guilty for inviting him to the wedding.

Sylvia then took over. "The great news is that we fell in love and wish to be married as soon as it can be arranged."

It was Jenna who exclaimed, "well it's about time, we all knew this day would come. So, let's have a party, heh!"

Max had always known that it was difficult to come into and leave this world, but birth and death was nothing compared to preparing for a wedding. The entire long week was divided with everyone being given job to complete. Bess Adams was given the job of hand writing, in fancy calligraphy, some fifty invitations. Grant had to deliver each one individually. Everyone had to go to Stevenson's Mercantile and buy a new suit or dress for the occasion. Jenna had to lead the detail to decorate the parish hall. Nellie, worked with Kate's Diner to choose and prepare dinner for 90 guests. Along with Bess, they did the alterations necessary to dresses and or men's suits. Elmer Adams had to rent a carriage to bring the bride to the church and arranged for parking buggies and individual horses. Finding a worker to watch the horses was difficult since most of the merchants and their employees would be at the wedding.

Initially, it appeared that Max and Brian would not be assigned a task to complete. It was Max who told Brian that the family would need to be vigilant in preventing revenge or retribution from old bounty hunting days or from Juan Guerra. It was Brian who took a trip along the Valley's eastern trail. He hired several men, who had experience with a rifle or pistol, to be present the wedding day. Each man was informed as to where his position would be, and each was paid $20 for their service.

Meanwhile, at the Big Mug Saloon, a patron was drinking heavily and babbling. Standing at the bar, another patron asked him what he was doing in town. The stranger said, "I'm here for a special occasion, and for me to get my revenge for my brother's death." The information went over the other patron's head, but the bar-keep caught on its meaning and thought, *the only special occasion that I know of is the Cassidy/Adams wedding and Max would be the man at risk of deadly retribution.* The next morning, the bar-keep passed on this intelligence to Sheriff Silvers.

The next day, Wes met with Brian and Max, to set up a secure wedding day. Wes related the bar-keep's info and Max was not surprised. After a good meeting it was agreed that Wes and his three deputies would be armed an appear to direct traffic—when keeping their eyes open for unwanted guests. Grant, Elmer, Brian and Max would be armed with a Webley Bulldog in a shoulder holster under their dress vests. The hired men, with rifle expertise, would be placed on nearby roof-tops overlooking the church and parish hall. Several pistol armed men would be stationed in several key locations, such as all door entries to the church and parish hall. All these men wore a temporary special deputy's badge and two were always close to the bride and groom—as their private security detail. Once the details were agreed upon, Brian said, "are we overdoing it with all this fire power. Our guests will start getting nervous."

"This is one time that overkill is acceptable. I don't want to lose a family member or guest because we are not prepared."

The wedding day finally came, and everything was going according to plan. Max and Brian were impatiently waiting at the altar for the organist to start playing "here comes the bride." Once the Adams', Jenna, and Nellie were seated, the music started. Grant appeared with Sylvia on his arm and walked down the aisle. Max lost all track of time as he stared in his beautiful wife's eyes. It was clear to him that he was making the wisest decision of his life. A life with Sylvia and her dream.

After the official ceremony, people were trying to gather in front of the church, but Wes and his entourage escorted everyone to the security of the parish hall. After the reception line was exhausted, everyone sat down to a traditional meal of chicken pie with vegetables, white gravy and dumplings. Dessert was the wedding cake and ice cream. The latter surprised the guests. They all wondered how Kate's Diner could keep the ice cream from melting.

After the meal, dancing started and lasted till late afternoon. When it came time for the newlyweds to leave, Wes commented that Max's cost for security had been a waste of money. Max added, "the party is never over till the fat lady sings. In this case, the party is over when I close the door to the bridal suite at the Winslow Hotel."

With final goodbye's being said, people were moving outside to see the newlyweds off on their honeymoon. When Max appeared in the doorway with Sylvia, a loud rifle shot was heard from high above. As everyone looked up to a nearby roof, a man came plunging down to the ground as another rifleman waved to the crowd—that man was a local homesteader hired by Brian by the name of Wilbur Haggerton.

Finally getting to the Winslow Hotel, as Max closed the door to the bridal suite he said, "this is the day I've been looking forward to since I met you weeks ago." Sylvia responded by placing her hands around his neck and passionately kissing him. Afterwards she said, "don't talk, time to make love. We have all week to talk, but not tonight!"

Their first time at unrestricted intimacy went slowly. When both were maximally aroused, Max said, "show me or tell me what you want."

Sylvia did not hesitate and made their first copulation nearly painless. After both reaching their nirvana, they lay breathless and sweaty, but for a short time when their passions again came to life. It was a repeated episode and each time was a more complete fusion of the body and soul. By morning, they both enjoyed a hot bath in their private water closet. They finally went downstairs for an absolutely needed 'replenishing' breakfast of steak, eggs, biscuits and coffee. Although, they had plans for the day, those plans were delayed till the next day as the couple returned to their den for private activity. By dinnertime, they both returned to the hotel restaurant for a 'replenishing' dinner of prime rib, baked potatoes, carrots and coffee. Dessert was apple pie with cheese. After dinner, they needed a walk to digest their food, but elected to forgo the walk till tomorrow. They both had a more pleasant alternative to an aimless "walk without a destination."

The next day, after private time and a good breakfast, Max finally said that they had some business to take care of. Their first stop was Stevenson's Mercantile. Max asked Elmer, "I owe Wilbur Haggerton for saving my life. Does he have an account that I can make a deposit to and provide him a credit?" Elmer looked confused as he pulled out his credit ledger. "Wilbur is having a tough time to feed his family this year. He owes me $79 and it goes up weekly. He's like many homesteaders, they are poor and most have a small money crop that generates income, but it's not enough to pay their bills here for food and clothing essentials. Yet, I can't refuse them, they are all my friends and I want them to survive."

Well Mr. Stevenson, here is a voucher off our bank for $250. Pay off his bill, give him more vittles than he asks, two boxes (OO buck and #6 bird shot) of shotgun shells for hunting, a change of clothes for each family member, and anything else he needs."

"But Mr. Adams, I don't think he has a shotgun"

"Well, he has a rifle since he used it to save my life. So, add two boxes of 44 ammo and give him a shotgun with a scabbard for hunting. Also, how many Valley homesteaders, from town to two miles east of my parents, have an unpaid balance?"

Elmer said, "let me do some quick ciphering……there are fourteen with a total balance on credit of $912."

"Ok, here is another voucher for $1,500. I'm sure you can find other families that need some help."

"Oh my, do I tell them who the benefactor is?"

"Only tell Wilbur and swear him to secrecy. The others must not know. If they hesitate to accept the funds because homesteaders are very proud, make it clear that several others will get the same gift, and no one will ever know. Emphasize gift, not charity, heh!"

"Great, I assure you that I will keep careful books for you to check."

"When the money runs out, mention it to me and we'll see what can be done. On second thoughts, I'm a firm believer in giving people a means to feed themselves. So, make sure that every family has a hunting shotgun with ammo, ammo for their rifle, fishing accessories and all the seeds they need for their vegetable gardens. So, please start a separate account for this self-survival project and here is a third voucher of $750 to fund that account. At the bank start two accounts—one labeled benefactor account and the other labeled survival account. Place my name with yours as holders of each account. And from now on, my name is Max and this is Sylvia."

"Yes, and my name is Elmer. Thank you for such unselfish generosity."

As they were leaving the store, Sylvia said, "are you sure you can afford this. That's a $2,500 fortune you're giving away?"

"When I quit the bounty hunting trade, I promised myself that I would give a portion of the rewards to people who needed it. Today, I found the place to make a difference to my neighbors."

Sylvia still had a doubtful look on her face

as Max said, "next stop is the bank, we need to establish a joint personal account. This account will separate our personal funds from the family's business account.

"Speaking of that, how do we divide the business income"

"By adding me to the family, we are now six workers and three families to receive equal income from the profits."

"Yes, that works out fine since the assets were always based on a one third basis."

"As far as equalizing assets, I have a plan for that when the time comes."

Arriving at the Merchant's Bank, they went to a teller. Sylvia asked to add Max to the family business account. When Max went to sign, he noticed that the account balance was $1,250. Max asked the teller to add an equal amount from his personal account. After signing and receiving a receipt. Max asked to add Sylvia to his personal account. When handed the account to Sylvia for signing, Sylvia nearly dropped the paper. She looked at Max and mouthed, "$49,341. Are you friggin kidding me?"

"Just sign your name, and don't forget, it's Sylvia Adams, heh."

As they left the bank, they headed to the land/ property tax office. On route on the boardwalk, Sylvia said, "Max why are you joining the family business, you could easily live off your bank account's interest or invest in land around town with even greater yields."

"High finance is not me. I want to work and live with my family. Money is always useful but doesn't bring happiness. You have to make yourself happy and being content with your work and family is the first step to happiness."

"Well then, helping your local homesteaders was a real good start. I promise you, we won't flaunt the money. We'll use it for our comforts, growing our business, and maintaining the benefactor fund."

In the land office, Sylvia changed her maiden name to her married name on the deed and tax papers. Adding Max to the deed and tax documents needed the signature of all present owners. Sylvia took the necessary forms and also took a copy for Jenna. This sensitive subject would eventually be discussed.

Their next stop was Emerson's Hardware. The owner, Floyd, greeted them. Max started.

"we are wondering what is new in planting and cultivating equipment?"

"Wow, this is serendipity! I passed the word out at your wedding and forgot all about telling you. I have received several new implements and accessories for older models. The salesman is arriving tonight and will set the items up in the morning. We are having a demo show starting at 1PM and you can place an order after the show."

The next stop was "Caldwell's Feed and Seed" store. Stepping inside, they were greeted by the owner, Parker. "That was a great wedding you had, the Missus and I were glad to be present. So, what brings you here on your honeymoon?"

Max took the lead, "I would like to deposit $1,000 to the family account to cover the seeds needed for next season."

"Certainly, glad to accept it, but your credit is good in my store."

"But, it's important for Grant Cassidy to see the deposit made on this day."

"Got'cha, Mr. Adams."

"Please call us Max and Sylvia," as a smile and nod followed.

Being early for dinner, they decided to visit the

hotel bar till the restaurant opened. Sitting in the bar, they took a table and ordered a bottle of red wine. As they were drinking and enjoying their private company, another couple entered. To their surprise, the lady wiped the chair's seat before the man sat down. She then unwrapped a cigar, cut the tip and even lit it before giving it to her apparent employer. Sylvia was getting disturbed by the goings on. When the lady sat, back to back, at an adjoining table, is when Sylvia lost it. "I thought slavery was outlawed decades ago?"

Max softly added, "look, they have matching wedding bands. I think that's his wife."

If it wasn't for the restaurant opening, Sylvia was about to add her two cent's worth. As it was, everyone in the bar entered the restaurant and all seemed forgotten, till the odd couple sat next to Max and Sylvia. Again, this couple sat, back to back, at adjoining tables. When the man's coffee arrived, the apparent wife got up to add sugar and cream to his coffee cup. When it came to order, the man was told the menu on a weekday night was a single item: meatloaf, mashed potatoes, peas and gravy. The man was not happy but let it slide and ordered two meals but with the gravy on the side.

Max and Sylvia ordered the daily special and waited with coffee. As the dinners arrived, the odd couple was served first as in the sequence the orders were taken. After the two plates were served, the gravy was placed next to the lady. As soon as the waitress left, the man started pounding the edge of the table with his knife.

Sylvia was steaming as she added, "if that was my husband, that table would turn to sawdust before I'd get up to serve that creep."

Max was trying not to laugh, but it was difficult to carry a straight face. Fortunately, the lady got up and brought the gravy along and poured it in the man's plate. Suddenly, the man gets up and slaps his apparent wife in the face, saying, "you know, I don't like gravy over my potatoes. When are you going to learn?" The wife held her face, poured gravy over the meatloaf and sat down.

Sylvia looked at Max, and no words were spoken. Max got up, walked behind the odd man, and said, "sir, it takes an ass and an idiot to treat your wife like you do. Without hesitation, he put his hand on the back of his head and slammed the man's face three times in the plate of food. The last thrust showed several teeth missing, peas coming out of his flattened nose, gravy and mashed potatoes all over his face. To complete the assault, Max poured the remainder of the gravy over the man's head and covered his hair with gravy. As he picked the man off his chair, he walked him quickly to the door and literally threw him off the boardwalk onto the street full of horse manure.

Coming back into the restaurant, he says to the wife, "Ma'am, if you wish to divorce this animal, I will pay for the attorney, court fees, put you up in the hotel with meals till the divorce is final. Then I'll send you by train to San Antonio to a lady friend who will accept you at my word. She will put you up in her boarding house and employ you in her legitimate business. Now enjoy your dinner and stay in the hotel at my cost tonight. Let me know your decision in the morning, we can meet in the lobby by breakfast time."

Max and Sylvia had a quiet dinner and retired to their suite for the evening. By morning, they were totally exhausted from their antics. Max had a thought. "I'll be the first to admit, that I just cannot get enough of you." "Oh really, well why is it that I feel I'm always begging for more?"

"Ok, well I'm certain that this is a lustful drive

from abstinence as a young adult. I bet if we put a bean in a jar every time we have relations during our first year of marriage, we would then spend a lifetime emptying the jar if we removed a bean every time we had relations after this first year." *Little did Max know that Sylvia already had twelve matchsticks separated, and counting, that would be converted to the bean jar once they got home!*

Arriving in the lobby, the abused wife was there. She got up and said, "my married name is Virginia McElvey and my maiden name is Nichols. I wish to become Miss Nichols if you will help me." Sylvia said, "come have breakfast with us and we'll spend the morning getting things set up for you." "Before you agree, you need to know that my husband is owner of the 'King of Spades Saloon' in town, and he is a very powerful and vindictive man." "So be it, you have warned us."

Spending time with one of the town's attorneys, the Adams learned that Edwin McElvey had assets over $20,000. It was Max who suggested a quick divorce if he offered Virginia a financial settlement of $5,000—equal to $1 per day plus the balance for mental anguish and physical abuse, for the past ten years. Without children, there would be no alimony. If he did not accept the settlement, the divorce would be dragged on till his assets would be cut in half.

That afternoon, they went to the implement show. There were approximately a dozen people in attendance. After the presentation, people went around looking at old and new items. Sylvia mentioned to Max, "we have all the standard implements, I'm interested in accessories, modifications and new items. The first they checked out was a way to add water to seeds during the planting stage—promoting early and consistent germination. The salesman explained, "after the seeder drops the seed, water can be added to the seeded furrow before the seeds are buried and the ground compacted. You can adjust the sprinkling holes to control the amount of water dropped, and the tank holds 20 gallons. It can be mounted on any model of row seeders."

The next item of interest was a steering mechanism for in-between row tilling. The salesman added, "this simple blade is attached to the front of a tiller. When the horse gets too close to the plants, the tiller will also get too close and may damage the plants. The rider can leave the horse to vary his position because with a slight pull right or left of the blade control, the tiller will follow the angle of the buried blade.

The next new item was an eye catcher. A shredder or grinder of vegetable leaves, stems, roots and some actual vegetables. They both remembered the salesman's presentation. "This machine allows you to turn any plant material into short one-inch pieces. The quicker you return the plant material to the earth, the quicker the decomposition. To accomplish this, attach this shredder over the manure spreader. When finished shredding, spread the load onto your land and follow it with a finish harrow to bury the plant material. If you let the shredded plant material dry in the sun, it will take longer for the minerals and organic material to be available for use." Sylvia said to Max, "we need this machine because manure and phosphate is expensive and plant parts are free. We'll even dispose of post mature or rotting vegetables instead of storing them for the pig farmer to pick them up—and stink up the premises till they are picked up, heh."

The last item was another accessory to fit on their seeder. The salesman explained, broadcasting phosphate is very expensive and feeds the growth of weeds. The grower needs to place fertilizer where the plants are, not in-between rows where irrigation occurs. This dispenser will drop a row of phosphate ahead of the furrow blade. That way when the seeded furrow is covered with dirt, the phosphate will be a top dressing for plant use—not for weeds to use.

Max said, "it seems to me that we need all these accessories and a shredder. Are there any implements that we should double up on?"

"I'm not sure, the University teachers kept emphasizing that once the seeds are in and irrigation follows a regular schedule, the real work to get a good crop is tilling and hilling up the rows of many plants. That can require the work of several men and extra implements. I would hate to find out in mid-season that we needed an extra tiller and hilling crow-wings."

"There is one surprise that I never mentioned. By next season, we will need to buy the neighbors manures. That means hauling manure and this will not be efficient with our 16 cubic foot manure spreader. There is a new 'mega' machine that holds 50 cubic feet of manure and requires four work horses to activate the spreader in the field."

When Sylvia mentioned this to the salesman, he pointed out that manufacturing for this mega machine will not start till January. If they placed an order today, they would be first to get one, and if not needed, the order could be cancelled anytime. Sylvia placed the order without a deposit.

"What is the estimated cost of these items?

Sylvia looks at the brochures, "watering adapter $42, phosphate adapter $49, tiller steering adapter $38, shredder $219, tiller with steering adapter $176, hilling crow-wings $117, freight to the farm $22. That comes up to a total of $663."

"Pay the man with a voucher from our account."

"But, that's your money!"

"No, from now on, my money and your money is our money."

That night was their last one at the Winslow. They had dinner with Virginia McElvey Nichols and found out that her husband had accepted the financial settlement and wanted an immediate non-contested divorce. Max had already telegraphed his friend and she would be expecting her anytime. In the morning, Max paid the attorney's fees, gave Virginia a train ticket to San Antonio, gave her a permission slip to buy a new wardrobe at Elmer's store and gave her $50 in cash.

Afterwards, they would head home. Sylvia would take the lead and soon start planting seeds in the field. Max was going to start his one-year apprentice. *Little did either know, that a man who pretended to be a customer at the implement show, and was now in the Winslow restaurant, was actually the brother of a well-known outlaw who had died on the gallows—thanks to those bounty hunters, Silvers and Adams. Revenge was only days away.*

***

CHAPTER 12—The Apprentice Year

Arriving at the homestead, the newlyweds were surprised to see a major construction project in progress. When Grant was asked what was going on, he said. "Nellie and I went to town to discuss the building of a second house to handle all these newlyweds. When the Adams' got a whiff of this idea, the project escalated to two houses. Before we knew it, it included a new barn between the two houses. Finally, the contract was finalized. Each house would include a new windmill well, water closet and hot water for a hot bath."

"But why?"

"It's our wedding presents to the four of you from the four of us."

Work had stopped for the day and party time had started. It ended with a banquet for dinner, put on of course by Nellie and Bess. As bedtime approached, Max and Sylvia retired to Sylvia's bedroom. Max said, "now we are not in an insulated bridal suite. So, no squealing, groaning or yelping during our love making."

"Now that you know what happens to me when you get into 3rd gear, I guess you'd better stay in 2nd gear, heh?"

Max just lost it, pillows were flying, Sylvia was yelling and running around the room, over the bed and trying to lock herself in the closet, but not succeeding. They were both laughing out loud and that got the listening ears to do the same. Eventually, someone yelled, "lights out, it's quiet time, we have a lot of work to do tomorrow." And quietly, their love-making finished—in 3rd gear.

***

The next morning, under Grant's tutelage, Max learned how to harness work horses. He was then shown how to plow virgin ground. It took a while to get the hang of controlling the depth of each furrow. After three days and some ten acres cultivated, Max spent three more days disc and finish harrowing the new plot of land. Max was a bit lame from sitting behind a horse, all week, bouncing on a steel seat and directing horses and adjusting equipment.

All week, Max would collapse into bed and

immediately fall asleep. The sixth night, Max tried to pull off the same stunt, but Sylvia would have none of it. She said, "tonight you have three gears and you're going to use them, or you're fired from the apprentice position!"

The next morning, after a replenishing breakfast, the family went to church. Max was wearing his Colt, and Sylvia had her Bulldog in her reticule. Grant and Brian were both carrying a Bulldog in a shoulder holster as well. Everyone had been warned to stay alert and look for any unusual faces giving off a furtive look.

Max had spotted an individual across the street from the church. He was wearing a brown shirt, canvas beige pants, a dirty brown hat, and his clothing looked slept in and filthy. With a five-day beard and a hung-over look, he looked rather scruffy. As Sheriff Silvers was approaching the post-sermon gathering, the observer disappeared.

"Howdy Wes, how's life treating you as sheriff?"

"Pretty well, this is a great little town and it's growing fast, Meg is liking it here and we're thinking of building a house. Meg got a job helping the needy and is paid by the county coffers. She's very happy. Now enough visiting,

I need to warn you. There is talk in the local saloons of some smelly and scruffy drunk making threats against me and you. It's just 'talk', so I can't arrest him."

"I already spotted him on the street a few minutes before you arrived. He is certainly scruffy looking, and I'll likely smell him before he drygulches me. But I'll be on the lookout and warn the family. Thanks for the warning, and you be careful as well, heh."

As per tradition, the entire family went to Kate's Diner for a brunch meal. The place was mobbed mostly from church attendees. After their meal, everyone got to spend Sunday afternoon doing their own hobbies or interests. Sylvia and Max went to the range to practice pistol and long-range rifle shooting. The loud gunshots got Grant, Brian and Jeanna to join them. Since Nellie did not cook on Sundays, it was up to Sylvia and Jenna to put on the evening dinner meal. Today was their specialty, roast pork slow cooked all day, with mashed potatoes, gravy, carrots and buttered home-made bread.

Just before dinner was served, Max asked Sylvia in private, "what do I owe you for such a lavish Sunday dinner?"

"A silent third gear," was all she softly said with a wide smile.

The next three days, Max appeared to have it easy. He was driving the team of horses, as Sylvia and Brian were working the seeder. One was working the watering and or the phosphate applicators, the other was working the furrowing and burying of seeds. It was a delicate process but all three got use to the three jobs. Max got to do the other two jobs, and everyone got to drive the horses—in a straight line.

At the end of the third day, all three workers felt good at mastering this seeder. They had planted seeds ranging from leaf lettuce, carrots, beets, spinach, radishes, rutabaga, and onions—the regions early cold crops. As they were putting away the horses and the equipment, a rider was pulling in the yard at a fast clip. Max recognized him as Wes's deputy, Sam Conover.

"What is going on Sam?"

"Wes has been shot and is in bad shape. He's with Doc Murphy and wants to see you immediately. He took a bad shot to the chest and........well, please come right away."

Brian helped Max saddle his horse, as Max

went to get his gear. They rode off and were in town 15 minutes later. Entering Doc's office, they were met at the door by Emily Murphy, the Doc's wife and nurse. "The doctor is still adjusting some tubes and bottles, but you may go in."

As Max entered the room, all he saw was rubber tubing coming out of Wes's chest. The tubes were going to bottles of water, some of blood and some of bubbling water. Doc Murphy spoke up, "learned how to manage chest wounds in the Civil war and the Indian wars. This is a homemade contraption that sucks out blood and traps air that would collapse his lung. I have sewed the entrance and exit wound, and if we don't get an infection and he awakens, Wes will survive."

Under his breath, Doc Murphy said, "I only wish I had the money to buy some of the modern medical inventions that would save lives. Guess I'll have to continue improvising for now."

Max stayed at Wes's bedside as he woke up two hours later. Wes finally gave his story. "I was on my evening walk-thru when someone standing in an alley, called me out. As I turned and drew, he fired. I never had a chance. Took a hit in the chest and then passed out."

"Any idea who shot you?"

"It was that scruffy fella we had talked about. No one knows his name, but I suspect it was a revenge shooting, and I suspect you're next on his list. Be careful."

"If he's after me, then he's still in town. I'll find him."

Max visited the saloons in town. He wasn't in the "Wet Bucket" or in "McClouds Tavern, the last saloon was McElvey's "King of Spades." As he walked thru the batwing doors, McElvey yells out, "get out, you're not welcome in here."

Max shouts back, "shut up, or you'll lose more teeth." As he turns to look at the patrons, he spots the scruffy one who was holding a pistol in his hands and pointing it at Max. Max made a lightning draw, fired and shot the pistol out of the outlaw's hand. He then stepped up to the man and said, "Mr. you stink, and keep your mouth shut, your breath smells like you are breathing thru your butt hole. Barkeep, I need a bar of lye soap." Max then punches the scruffy twice to knock him down. He then grabs the bar of soap, holsters his gun, grabs scruffy by the belt and drags him outside. There he throws him in the horse water trough and dunks him three times.

Scruffy was choking and coughing. Before he realized it, he found his clothing ripped off. Max then said, “start scrubbing or I’ll beat you to death, you filthy animal.”

When Max was satisfied scruffy was relatively clean, he grabbed him by the hair and dragged him to the sheriff’s office in his birthday suit. There he threw him in a cell and asked him who he was and why he had shot Sheriff Wes. When the answer was, “go to hell,” Max stepped into the cell with a Marlin nail in hand. As he pushed it up into a molar. Scruffy had a major convulsion and seemed to pass out. When revived, as he saw the nail coming at him again, he decided to say, “my name is Silas Hosmer, brother of Homer, who you hung for kidnapping and murder.”

“Well, Sheriff Silvers had better live, because you’ll never hang, I’ll beat you to death myself. And that is a promise.”

Max went back to Doc Murphy’s. Sylvia was there waiting for him. She never spoke but held his hand and waited for Max to speak.

“Doc, I heard you whisper to yourself something about needing modern medical tools and medicines. What do you need, and can you really save someone from a gunshot to the chest or save a woman from bleeding to death after delivery?"

"With the right equipment and medicines, I can save quite a few. But that means I need a clean operating and delivery room, modern steel surgical equipment, delivery forceps, and hundreds of medicines and other medical supplies."

'You'll have it. Keep your house as your office and your living quarters. Have an attached extension built to get your operating and delivery room as well as some patient rooms—all with running cold and hot water. Go see Mr. Thabo at the construction company. He is presently building me a house but get your plans ready since he'll be available within a week. Call it 'Murphy's Valley Hospital' and tell Mr. Thabo that I'll pay for it."

Doc Murphy was standing in a frozen position, it was his wife that said. "well doc, this man just gave you your hospital. Look alive and say thank you."

Max and Sylvia spent the next two nights at the Winslow Hotel. The third day, when the Adams entered Wes' room, they saw that the rubber tube was clamped, the bottles were not bubbling, and the blood bottle was empty. Wes explained, "if my lung does not re-collapse or re-bleed, the tube comes out in 24 hours. I'm beginning to think that I may actually live thru a shot in the chest."

Sylvia added, "thanks to the competence of a great physician."

The next day, Wes's tubes were removed, and his right chest did not need further intervention. His lung was healing, and it was time for Max and Sylvia to return to the homestead. Spring planting time was here, and the transplants needed to go in the ground.

***

It was a concerted effort of several workers to get these transplants in the ground. A horse driver to keep a straight line equally spaced from the last row, and wide enough to allow tilling in the future. One man to pull the plants out of the pots and push them in the furrows. One man to heavily water the pots before they left the greenhouse. One man as carrier of transplant trays to the field by wagon. One man to provide food and water for the horses and the men. The worse job was sitting on the rear of the planter and directing the roller to press down the earth carefully around each transplant.

The only job that was permanent was Nellie's. She handled the watering of each pot before leaving the greenhouse. The other five workers rotated every hour, so in a ten-hour day, they did each job twice. To get the several thousand transplants in the ground took three full ten-hour days. At the end of each work day, after a warm bath and a hot meal, Sylvia and Max simply collapsed into bed. Sylvia finally said, "I finally understand, I wouldn't be able to find 1st gear if my life depended on it." Max just chuckled as he added, "yes dear, let's stay in neutral," as he rolled over and fell asleep.

The next morning a cold snap was in the making. The seeds they planted ten days ago were just breaking ground. More than likely, they should be able to survive near freezing temperatures. However, in case of a killer frost which would wipe out the germinating crop, it was elected to put the two-winged implements at work and cover the tender plants with a thin coat of dirt.

For ten hours, the two crow-winged implements never stopped, a rider would exchange himself and his team of horses for another man/horse team every two hours. By nightfall the multiple rows were all covered. In the morning, for the next three days, patchy areas of frost were noted over the planted fields—a rare occurrence in south Texas.

For the next sixty days, everyone was busy in the field taking care of growing plants. Two tillers, two crow-winged machines and continuous irrigation kept the six workers busy. The greenhouse in the summer was reserved for growing tomatoes. Although the tomato crop was evenly divided between the greenhouse and the open field, for unknown reasons the tomatoes did better in the greenhouse.

When the transplants came to maturity, the harvesting and marketing aspects came to life. The early harvest required picking and choosing of the mature plants. After the six family members picked most of one day, they had the two display wagons and two large transport wagons full of the winter crops started in the greenhouse. It was then, that Grant said, "we don't have time to pick the vegetables, we need to bring them to market. We need to hire some help in the field and leave the selling and marketing to us—the owners."

Max added, "and we need to expand our markets. This week, Sylvia and I will go to town, four miles west, and try to sell both our wagons. Brian and Jenna are going east, with two wagons, to a town some eight miles away. Assuming we sell 100% of our goods, I have computed, at the value of vegetables by the pound, to be anywhere from one to four bits per pound (a bit is 12 and a half cents). Volume sales are based by the full or half bushel. For example, a full bushel of potatoes sells for 8 bits, or +-$1 US. My computation yields a value of each wagon at +-$40--50, or $160--200 per week for six workers minus expenses and investment. That's a good start, but it's not enough"

Sylvia asks, "what is not enough. I'd say that is good income for our family!"

"I meant, that is not enough of a market. Look at the fields you have of vegetables approaching maturity."

Grant chimed in, "I saw this problem when we finished the first seeding. I have a food supplier in Brownsville, named 'Smithback Foods,' that will take whatever we send him. I've had a carpenter build us transport boxes that measure 2X2X2 square feet, or eight cubic feet. Each box has two long boards attached to the box that allows two or four men to handle the load. I have twenty boxes ready at Thabo's factory, ready for pickup."

"Great, let's get these boxes today, start loading them and send a trial load to Smithback. We'll send ten boxes and keep ten boxes here for the next load. On the return trip, Smithback will send us the empty boxes. Better still, have Mr. Thabo build us another 20 boxes. We may need to find another wholesaler possibly in Laredo—the other city accessible by water ferry."

Sylvia added, "now we need help. Let's hire some American or Mexican workers. The going wage is $1 per day with room and board included. That means, we need to build a bunkhouse and cook shack, and hire a cook. The cook would relieve us girls from the cooking chores after working all day on the business."

All agreed. Grant walked over at the construction site, stopped the workers saying, "we need an emergency bunkhouse and cook shack. Leave the houses and move over to the bunkhouse future site."

Within two weeks, things progressed quickly. The vegetables were maturing on schedule, Grant had sent his first load to Smithback, and the farmer's markets were already popular. Two tag-along wagons were added to the two neighboring towns, making this a caravan of three wagons arriving at each of the farmer's market. The display wagon was pulled by two geldings, but the double wagons were pulled by two Percherons.

A message was received thru the returning water ferry from Brownsville. The message stated, "the produce was fresh and of superb quality. Send more, ASAP. Your empty crates will return with each load and a bank voucher will be sent back via the ferry's Captain."

Grant had been conducting interviews while the bunkhouse was under construction. He ended up hiring six new workers. Three Mexicans married men that would work five days a week, stay in the bunkhouse at night, but go home on weekends to take care of their homestead. The three Americans were single men. The two older ones were permanent fixtures in the bunkhouse and cook shack and would usually work six days a week. The younger American was carousing in the town saloons on weekends but managed to return to the bunkhouse by Sunday evenings.

Things were moving along smoothly for two weeks in a row. Upon Brian and Jenna's return, they admitted having a problem with an overbearing gunfighter that would pick up vegetables but would leave without paying. Max knew that this meant trouble and gave customers the wrong impression. He offered to switch routes with Brian and the next week, they headed some 8 miles east to the next town.

The day was going well, and by 2PM, they were down to the bottom half of the third wagon. Max caught the appearance of someone with the swagger of an arrogant gunfighter. The man chose potatoes, tomatoes, onions, and turnip to supplement a beef stew. He then gave the produce to two of his toadies and they started to walk away. Max softly said, "Sir, you forgot to pay for your vegetables."

"Guess your friend last week didn't tell you we don't pay."

"Well, if you are in need and are hungry, I will give you all the food you need. I don't believe that's the case here." So, after doing a quick computation, he said, "you owe me 2-4-6-8 bits, or $1.

The gunfighter, now twisting up his upper lip, drew his pistol and even pulled back the hammer. "My name is Buster Page, and as I said, we don't pay."

Max reacted so fast that the gunfighter was stunned as Max placed the thumb-first finger web of his left hand directly wedged between the gunfighter's hammer and pistol frame. When the gunfighter pulled the trigger, the hammer fell onto Max's hand web. At the same time, Max drew his Colt and smacked the man in the forehead with the tip of the pistol barrel. Buster collapsed to the ground. His two toadies dropped the vegetables and went for their gun, as Sylvia pulled out her Bulldog from her shoulder holster and simply said, "drop those pistols back in their holsters or you're getting a bullet in the kneecaps."

With the episode defused, Max took $2 from the gunfighter's pocket—payment for two weeks. He then dragged the piece of crap and dropped him head first behind the Percheron horses—directly on top of the real fresh manure. Max's last trick was to unload the man's pistol, and then smashed and broke off the hammer against the wagon wheel's steel rim.

At the end of the day, Sheriff Peterson, arrived at the farmer's market. When told the day's event with Buster Page, he came to investigate. Max and

Sylvia were closing up. The two toadies were tied to the wagon wheel and Buster was still sleeping off the manure pile. Sheriff got the story from Max and said, "I've heard about you and glad to finally meet you. Now, the problem will be when Buster wakes up, smelling like a horse's behind, and having a huge black and blue egg on his forehead. He's not going to be a happy camper!"

"What was I to do? Let him get away, kill him or try to teach him a lesson?"

"You did what you had to do for today. Next week, he'll be waiting for you. He will goad you into a gunfight, and you'll have to kill him in self-defense. Sad to say, but that's the method of our times. To save face, the gunfight will be held in public. Just remember, let him draw first, to guarantee a fair fight and self-defense. Also, have some of your family watch the event with rifles in hand, and watch the surrounding rooftops for his men."

"That could be the way it will happen, but I suspect he's a coward and a fake. I think he'll be on the trail next week and will bushwhack me with the help of his two toadies."

"If that's the case, don't take chances and take

them out before your wagons arrive at the ambush location."

The next week on the homestead was spend seeding the next crop. For three days, the family planted the replacement crop. The crops would be rotated and replanted on a proven schedule. This allowed a continuous weekly supply of all produce. The yield was so good, because of all the tilling and hilling, that they doubled their wholesale orders to Smithback Foods. Somehow, word got to Laredo, and a local food distributor showed up one day. He visited the farm and left with a contract similar to Smithback. This distributor was called "Washington Foods" and sold his products all over Laredo.

When the day came to head to the farmer's market, changes were made. The drivers would be Sylvia and Brian to the east, and Grant and Jenna to the west. Max would scout ahead and try to find the ambush site.

Max rode a half mile ahead of the wagons. The trail was flat and treeless. The only place to hide was the high banks of the Rio Grande, but that didn't leave any place to hide the horses. Suddenly Max had an epiphany. Thinking like an outlaw, *"If I wanted to set an ambush, how could*

I do it? At that spot, he saw a small homestead, and all became clear. An outlaw could take over the homesteaders, wait in the house till the target appeared on the trail. Since most homesteads were the average of one hundred yards from the trail, it would be an easy shot with a rifle.

Max changed his approach. He went back to talk to Brian and Sylvia. They agreed on a new system. The wagons would not approach a homestead unless a red bandana would appear next to the trail and ahead of the homestead. The wagons didn't move for an hour to give Max a head start.

Max approached the first two homesteads from the rear and other than scare a housewife half to death, found nothing of danger and placed the red bandana by the trail. The third homestead was different. Tied in the rear of the house, next to the kitchen door, were three horses. Max knew he had found Buster and his toadies.

Max sneaked up to the house, saw nothing in the kitchen but in the main room were the two toadies holding a pistol on the young homesteading couple and one man bracing a rifle in the broken window. He quickly analyzed the situation. He had two choices. One, walk right in and have a shootout. Presumably, one hostage would likely die. The only safe approach was to pick each one off using his scoped Win. 1876.

Before Max set off to position himself 300 yards away, he took precautions to prevent these men from getting away on their horses. Max went in the barn to set up a deterrence, and immediately found what would serve the purpose—large wolf traps.

Walking back to his horse, Max rode three hundred yards in the "front forty" and set himself up on a tripod to scope the front of the house. Once set up, he was looking for the rifle shooter, but could not locate him. Instead, he spotted a toady holding a pistol to a young woman's head. Knowing that a head shot, with a high-powered rifle, would cause the nerves to freeze in place, and would prevent the outlaw from pulling back the hammer or even pulling the trigger.

Max steadied the rifle, set the scope to 300 yards, slowed down his breathing and heart rate, let a breath out and squeezed the trigger. The bullet, traveling at 1500 ft. per second, was faster than the speed of sound. It made a small hole in the glass and smashed into the toadies face below the nose. The face collapsed rearward as the back of the head exploded and half the brain followed. The outlaw's gun fell on the floor without discharging and the outlaw was blown over on his back.

Buster was looking at his dead man without belief. He told his living toady, "I can't shoot him at 300 yards, and if we don't beat it, he's eventually going to pick us off. So, let's tie these two up and we'll bring the woman as a hostage. You sneak behind the house and barn to get our three horses as I keep watching to be certain he doesn't sneak up on us."

The toady took off and as he got to the barn, slowly opened the barn door and stepped in. Max swore later that he heard the snap of two traps going off in sequence and then followed by a scream from hell. Buster knew that his man was out of commission and that he had to take the initiative.

Buster stepped outside holding the hostage woman in front of him and yelled out, "if you don't get on your horse and leave, I'm going to shoot her."

Max was not about to take his eye off his scope. He was waiting for Buster to slip and give him a shot. Suddenly, Max saw the hostage grab her hair "bun" with both hands and pulled something out. As her "bun" fell apart, Buster screamed, stepped aside, and grabbed his eye. Max pulled the trigger and hit him in center mass. The impact lifted him off his feet and threw him backwards thru the door.

Arriving at the house, Max asked the lady what she had done to distract the outlaw. She said, "I saw how you shot the other man in the face, and I knew if I could distract this piece of crap, that you would take care of him."

"But how did you distract him so violently?"

"Look at his right eye, that's my hair pin in his eye."

"Ouch, hey!"

Arriving at the farmer's market, Brian and Sylvia took care of the sales while Max looked up Sheriff Peterson and reviewed wanted posters. Buster had a $500 reward and the two toadies had $200 rewards—all for robberies and murder in northern Texas. Max then went to the nearest livery to sell off the outlaw's horses. The hostler looked at the horses and said, "outlaws always seem to have the best of horses. These are large geldings and would make great work horses."

Max realized he had missed this finding. He said, "you're right, I'll keep them. Where can I exchange rifles and pistols for work harnesses?"

"Two blocks on the left, my brother has a gun and leather shop."

Max walked in, said hello and gave the owner three Win 73 rifles and three Colt 45's. "How much to trade for three work harness for large geldings. The owner looked the guns over and said, "they are dirty and need cleaning but appear in good condition. Would you be interested in an even trade?"

"Yes sir."

"It will take a week to fit the harnesses. Where are the horses now?"

"In your brother's livery, I'll pick up everything next week."

The remainder of Max's apprentice year was uneventful as far as the business went. The weather was mild with a nice amount of rain and irrigation was yielding bountiful crops. The markets were adequate to handle the volume of their crops.

During the year, both newlyweds entered their new homes. The anticipated revenges did not seem to occur. Regardless, Max and Sylvia continued to wear their Webley Bulldog pistols on their belts.

***

CHAPTER 13—
Business as Usual

The next week, at the Farmer's market, they ran out of eggs at noon. It was now clear that their 150 chickens were no longer capable of meeting the town's demands. By 2PM, as their supply was down to the last quarter, Max saw the opportunity to escape and run two errands.

His first stop was the hospital construction. The adjacent building was up, and the men were doing finish work inside. Doc Murphy showed him around and explained the function of every room.

"How long before you open up shop, and have you received all the new equipment you wanted?"

"Yes, and along the new surgical equipment, the Missus, Savannah, has gone to San Antonio and learned how to administer ether so we can get away from the dangerous chloroform. I'll be completely functional in one week. Now the bad news, Mr. Stevenson and Mr. Thabo are looking for you."

"Yes, I figured. Where are they?"

"Mr. Thabo is in his shop, building shipping crates for your company. Let's go and see Mr. Stevenson who ordered all my supplies and then we'll stop at Mr. Thabo's shop."

The new equipment, tools and supplies cost $579. The construction costs were another matter. Mr. Thabo said, "the building cost $1200, the gas lamps cost $200, the plumbing, well and water closets cost $500, the glassed shelving cost $300, doors and windows cost $400, coal heating stoves for $400, and other miscellaneous expenses for $200. $3,200 will cover it."

"Can you add a small barn in the back for visitors, for $300?"

"Yes, can do."

"Max handed him a $3,500 voucher and added, "not a bad price for a life-saving building."

Doc Murphy added, "I hope I can repay your generosity some-day."

His second stop was at Caldwell's Feed and Seed store. As he walked in the store, he saw a large sign saying, "150 young laying hens on sale—40 cents each."

Max went out back and saw a temporary chicken coop full of healthy chickens. He went inside and bought the lot with mash, oyster shells and 150 slotted cardboard boxes. He then ordered some lumber and hardware screening against predators. After paying the bill, he arranged for Parker Caldwell to make delivery arrangements with McClintock Freighting.

On their way home, discussing the chicken market, Sylvia said, "In this part of the country, our food supply consists of meat from beef, poultry or pork, beans, other vegetables or eggs. Eggs have become a popular breakfast food and are not easily available for people living in small towns. Our town customers are counting on us to bring them vegetables and eggs. Plus, we can always use chicken manure, heh?"

"Now, with the extra 150 layers, we have to build another 45 boxes stuffed with hay for chickens to lay eggs. We also have to set a rigid schedule of picking up eggs once or twice a day."

"Why so often?"

"For two reasons, one is to get them into the cold cellar as soon as possible. The second is to prevent a "clutch" from forming."

"What is that?"

"A clutch is a group of eggs, say six or more, that encourages a hen to sit on the eggs, keep them warm, till they hatch. This is brooding, or a natural incubator. The result is that heat ruins the freshness of eggs." Sometimes, a hen turns into a brooder and spends her days sitting on eggs. This is a problem and this hen needs to end up in the oven for dinner."

"What does the public expect and understand from the phrase, 'farm fresh eggs.'"

"From the chicken coop to the cold cellar, without washing them. If you wash them, a protective coating is removed, and without this coating air will enter and promote the egg's degradation."

We don't have a rooster in our coop, and I don't believe there is one in this new batch. Don't we need a rooster?"

"Hens continue laying eggs till they get past five years of age. You don't need roosters if you want to sell eggs. Customers don't want to crack an egg and find an embryo in the frying pan. You keep roosters around some selected hens if you want to raise chicks. Otherwise the only value to a rooster is on the dinner table."

"Do our customers come to the market for vegetables or for eggs?"

"I don't care, as long as they come and buy both, heh."

"So how did we do today?"

"We sold out all three wagons and made $140 dollars. Not bad for a week's work, and that's not counting, Brians load or the wholesaling we do each week with Smithback and Washington Foods. I'd say we have a sound and profitable enterprise on its way."

"Yes, but the work needed to maintain this production, week to week, is very demanding. The six of us are working at capacity. Let's not forget that your mom and dad are getting on in age and one of you ladies may get pregnant anytime."

"I know, and with our new homes with insulated bedrooms! Well you know what I mean."

"If I was deaf, I would still understand."

Sylvia just looked at him and gave him that inviting smile. Max paused and then asked, "would you be happy to be with child?"

"Oh yes, my life would be complete. My dream of owning a business, having a loving husband and several children would make me the happiest woman in the world."

Max thought, *"I'm beginning to understand*

why happiness is being content with your personal interests, work, and loving family.

***

The year's day to day became business as usual. The lack of physical revenge from outlaws allowed everyone to let their guards down and concentrate their efforts on working the farm. At the end of the year the first official business meeting was called to order by Sylvia.

The meeting started with all six family members present. Nellie was asked to proceed with a financial report. Nellie opened her ledger an began throwing out numbers. "The expenses included: labor, seed costs, implement repair, delivery wagons, shipping crates, shipping costs by river ferry, food costs, clothing replacement, hand tools, egg crates, and miscellaneous." Nellie put a number on each expense and the total did surprise everyone. Nellie added, "remember folks, it takes money to make money, and it's clear that labor expenses are overshadowed by much larger profits."

Nellie went on to income. Our income is based on the four distribution sites, the two retail farmer's markets in nearby towns, and the two wholesale destinations in Laredo and Brownsville. Nellie threw out the figures and everyone was amazed. Nellie then said, "Each family has had three distribution vouchers of $1,000 each. Allowing for a replacement and growth fund for the future, each family now gets the final voucher of the year." Nellie hands out three $5,000 vouchers to the men. Grant finally spoke up and said, "this is more money than any one deserves." Brian added, "that may be so, but we worked hard, and Jenna and I are proud to accept it."

Sylvia moved along to plans for the coming year and beyond. First of all are the numbers of our produce balanced or are we short of specific foods. Jenna answered, "at our farmer's market we are always short of fruits. Since we don't have tree grown oranges and grapefruits, our customers like watermelon and cantaloupe." Grant also supported this need from the wholesalers.

Sylvia added, "we need more Jalapenos peppers. Apparently, a sauce called salsa requires the hot peppers to produce the different grades of tanginess. In addition, there is now a request for 'sealed turnips.' This means that in the fall season, people are requesting that the turnips be coated with paraffin wax. This seals the skin from air or humidity and makes them last thru the winter months—especially for town's people without a root cellar."

Sylvia went to the last subject. "Do we expand the business or maintain the status quo?" Silence fell upon the group. Sylvia then added, "Max has good ideas about the options, and so I yield the floor."

Max started, "a thriving business must never accept the status quo. There's always something you can add or do, either in a major or minor way. Today, our problem is like Brian said, 'we worked hard this past year.' Now mom and dad are getting older, the gals may get pregnant, or anyone of us could get sick. Before we consider expanding our production. We need to split the fourteen-hour winter day into two seven-hour shifts—5AM to noon and noon to 7PM. The summer shifts could be extended to eight-hour shifts. To accomplish this, we need to hire six reliable employees that can take over the family's duties. That means several months of training. Once we have two shifts six days a week, we can cultivate new lands and find other wholesalers or other retail sites east of home."

"Nellie chimed in, "boy that sounds great, I didn't want to bring it up, but Grant and I agree with Max. We need personal time for ourselves."

Brian gave Jenna a nod. Jenna smiled and said, "well, considering I'm already twelve weeks pregnant, I'm all in favor as well." The meeting had an intermission to share tears and congratulations. Sylvia went back to the agenda and added, "I find there so much planning needed, that an afternoon off every day would give me the time to do what is necessary. We're also in favor of the double shift."

Brian asked, "who are we after to take over our jobs."

Max answered, "experienced homesteaders who live nearby and can ride to work every day. That way, they have half a day to do their own work and can still be home every night. Most important, these homesteaders can now bring home some cash every week, and we don't have to expand the bunkhouse."

Grant asked, "Max, give us an idea of what investment we need to do this expansion."

"I think we need;

1. The cook will need an assistant who can also do their own shopping.
2. Extra work horses.
3. We may need to expand the barn to house the extra work horses and the homesteader's horses.
4. New market. Retailing is twice as profitable as wholesaling. We need to get three new wagons so we can extend eastward into another town.
5. We'll need another 'mega' manure spreader since we'll be hauling manure from more distant ranches and homesteads.
6. We'll need to start buying more commercial phosphate.
7. The greenhouse will need expansion or build a second. Fall transplants is the one thing that allows us to maintain a year-round farmer's market.
8. And last, but not least and don't kill the messenger. We need to start selling canned vegetables to maintain our winter markets."

Paper spit balls and boos were all over the gathering. Eventually, Max was allowed to explain. "Winter produce can be skimpy, even if we still grow crops during the winter because of careful planning. If we only provided canned vegetables during the winter, our crowds would hold up during January and February."

Nellie asked, "and pray tell, who will be doing all this canning and processing—which is usually done in the summer when produce is plentiful, and the temperature is too hot to work over a hot stove."

"We'll build a summer outside kitchen to do the canning and processing, besides some vegetables will be pickled and not require processing. We have three large cold cellars to house these products till winter."

Jenna asks, "jars are expensive, how do we compensate for the cost?"

"Canned foods is for local retailing, we offer a buy back program for both egg crates and canning jars. That way no one pays for an item that is reusable."

Nellie added, "and again, who will do the work?"

"We'll hire it out, it takes money to make money. I'm certain that in these hard times, we should find American and Mexican housewives that would like to supplement their family income."

In addition, it advertises the fact that employment is available at the Cassidy homestead."

"Before I sit down, I have one last point to bring out. We need to advertise all our produce that leaves the farm to wholesale locations. Mr. Stevenson tells me that we can have a stamp made that applies edible ink to any vegetable. It would become our trademark—a one-inch **CIRCLE** with the letter **C** inside. For Cassidy, of course."

Silence followed Max's borderline controversial diatribe. Sylvia was not going to interrupt the moment, she was deep in personal thought *If Max and the others only knew that I missed my monthly and I think I may also be pregnant.* Minutes passed in deep thought when Grant, the family patriarch, got up. With a nod from Nellie, he said, "your mother and I are in complete agreement with Max's four suggestions: it's time to slow down, time to expand with help and investments, time to diversify with help, and it's time to advertise. I make a motion we accept these recommendations and move ahcad."

Brian got up, "I second the motion and would add a codicil, I propose we vote Max our General Manager for the next year."

"Wait, why me?'

Brian returned, "Because you have earned the respect of this family and our employees, and you have a vision for the future. To the outside world of commerce, you exhibit power and leadership. What else could we ask for? I'm so proud to have you as a brother-in-law."

Sylvia took over, "all those if favor of the motion and its codicil, please raise your hand." All five hands went up and Sylvia had a tear of joy in her eyes.

"Uh…...I was only kidding, right? Ok, I'll work on these four goals during the year, and we'll see where we are by the next annual meeting. No promises, but I'll do my best."

***

This was November and the beginning of a new fiscal year. The greenhouse, this time of year, was needed to plant seeds for the winter crop. However, the greenhouse was full of mature tomato plants that were still yielding fruit. Max made a quick decision and hired Thabo's construction company to dig an independent cold cellar covered by an insulated roof. Once completed, the tomato plants were pulled out with the roots intact and hung upside down in the cold cellar. Every other day, the root complex was sprinkled with water. The plants continued to produce tomatoes till February.

With the greenhouse empty, seeding started. While the three ladies were seeding in glass tubes, the construction company was busy expanding the greenhouse. It took ten days to expand the greenhouse, and the girls spent a month seeding and transplanting. In the end they ended up with 3,000 cold weather plants and 500 tomato plants.

During the month of green house work, Sylvia was not in a loving mood. She was obviously physically tired, and her mood was labile. Going to bed early was her routine, but that night Max was also tired and decided to follow her to bed after washing up. As he entered the bedroom, Sylvia was standing akimbo and totally nude.

Max said, "I'll never tire to see you wearing only your privates. You are just gorgeous. Now, is there a meaning behind this greeting?"

"Well, better enjoy this body now, because it's going to change. I'm pregnant," as she begins to cry.

Max walks up to her and gently takes her in his arms. "why are you crying, that's the most wonderful news and the greatest gift you could ever give me."

"Because, I'm so happy. Now make love to me."

Getting thru the winter and maintaining a farmer's market was a challenge. The vegetables they sold included cabbages, turnips, carrots, onions, potatoes, sweet potatoes, pumpkins, squash, all types of beans and peppers. All these items had been preserved in the new commercial cold cellar as well as the three private home cold cellars. The ladies had agreed that canned vegetables would be popular and did a last- minute canning of string beans, beets, corn, carrots, and some potatoes. They also managed to pickle all the last of the cucumbers and many beets as well. By the end of the late canning season, the cold cellars of each house and the new commercial cold cellar were full to the top.

The wholesale shipping to Laredo and Brownsville was changed to every other week during the winter months. This allowed the farmer's markets to continue. The fact that tomatoes continued into mid-February was hard to believe, but a welcome produce on the wagon. Egg production slowed down a bit, but with the well protected coal stove in the coop, a reasonable supply was regularly at hand.

The winter months allowed Max to advertise and start interviewing for full time field workers and canning ladies. One couple had a unique story. At the age of 50, the homesteader had a accident and ended up with a bad fracture in his thigh. He could not work for months and was forced to sell the farm and move into town. When the fracture failed to heal, he had to go to San Antonio for special surgery. Now, two years later, the leg has finally healed but they were now out of money. His wife was a homesteading wife who had canned everything out of her garden. The man had limitations that prevented his leg from bending or twisting. They were both hired, the man would work in the field as a cultivator/tiller behind a horse, and the lady would be in charge of canning. Realizing they were broke, Max gave them an advance of $100 to get them by till the job started.

The remainder of the interviews yielded more local homesteaders. It was easy to find several other husband and wife teams to cover both field work and canning. The mix was four American and two Mexican men for field work, and two

American and two Mexican women for canning. The canners would not start until June 1st, but the men would start by March 1st.

Hiring more field pickers was more difficult. Americans were not as interested as Mexican workers to work in the hot sun picking up vegetables for a dollar a day. So, the Mexican applicants saw the need and made Max a proposal. One Mexican would pick up a team of Mexican workers and bring them by wagon to the Cassidy homestead. These included both men and women. They would arrive by 8AM with water and their lunch. With an hour off for lunch, they would work straight thru till 6PM dinner was served. That would make a nine-hour work day with dinner included. Max signed an agreement that included a minimum of eight workers each day. The Mexican representative shook Max's hand and said, "please call me Tony, and a minimum of eight workers will not be a problem. At a 20 to 1 exchange rate with US funds, you'll find the workers vary from day to day since so many of our country-men need help. Yet, we will always give you 110% of our effort." The last person he hired was an assistant cook, who turned out to be Tony's wife.

The next step in getting all his ducks in a row was a trip into town to place orders. Living, without a railroad into your community, required long periods to get non-routine items. Max's first stop was Emerson's Hardware where he ordered a second mega manure spreader. In order to get it delivered within ten days, Max paid the extra fee. It was important to have it this winter, because it was the winter months when the pickers were delegated to hauling manure from nearby ranches.

His second stop was Stevenson's Mercantile. He ordered a cookstove, pint and quart canning jars, processing pots and a sink for cleanup. Plus, he ordered the company logo stamp with a supply of ink. At Caldwell's Feed and Seed store, he ordered three tons of commercial phosphate, as well as five hundred pounds of both magnesium and potassium supplements. This included delivery to the homestead.

At the livery, he arranged for Sammy to find him two more work horses and two more large geldings, all with new harnesses. His last stop was Thabo's Construction. Mr. Thabo greeted Max, "nice to see you Max, I always like to see my local 'cash cow' come thru the door." As he breaks into a roar but adds, "no insult intended, heh!'

"Good morning, I don't mind being your cash cow since you do good work at a fair price. Now today I need four items. I need to expand my barn to hold ten more horses. I will also need, by June 1st, a summer kitchen such as a one wall lean-to with water and a cookstove chimney. I will need three new wagons, one of which is a display wagon like you built last time. And, for last, I need some trays that will hold eight pint or quart canning jars."

"May I make a suggestion? Enlarging your barn for ten more horses will make it a dangerous fire hazard—if a fire starts, you'll never get all those horses out. Instead, let's move the new barn far away and use the same well for water. That way the closer barn would be for work horses and the other would be for riding horses. Besides, with the new wagons, you'll be glad to have the extra lean-to for wagon storage."

"Great idea, let's sign a contract, if you're done milking the cow!"

"Oops, I'll never use that line again. Anyways, my shop's team will start working on the wagons and canning jar trays. My field crew will be over to build a new barn and erect a summer kitchen. Thanks for the business, Max."

The winter was going well at the farmer's markets. Sylvia was over the morning sickness, was beginning to show, and had her first visit with Doc Murphy. Sylvia was looking forward to giving birth in the birthing room at the new hospital. The one new thing was that Doc Murphy had gone to San Antonio and learned how to perform a C-Section. This was TMI (too much information) to share with Max who was already worried about Sylvia continuing to work on the farm.

As per their routine, Max and Sylvia took off for their weekly run into the town's farmer's market. This season, they were only filling two wagons. The day started as usual, but with fewer vendors. By 1PM, they were almost sold out when two well healed gunfighters showed up and were seen collecting cash from all the vendors. When they got to Sylvia they said, "town council is charging a vendor's fee. $3 for the site and $3 for the extra wagon."

Sylvia was surprised and said, "I'll confirm that with the council and if it's true, I'll pay them directly."

As Sylvia turned to walk away, one of the men put a hand on her shoulder and turned her around, rather briskly. "Ma'am, we are collecting now, fork over the cash!"

Max was listening to the conversation as he was harnessing the team to the wagon. When he saw one hoodlum's hand on Sylvia's shoulder, he exploded in a rage. Jumping off the wagon's whiffle tree, Max landed on the man touching his wife. The surprised miscreant landed on his back and Max pummeled him repeatedly to the face while saying, "never ever put your hands on my wife again, do you hear me?" The limp body tried to respond with some grumbling but passed out before he could finish.

As Max was landing punches, his partner went for his gun. Sylvia had anticipated this move, as she pointed her Bulldog to the man's groin and said, "pull out your pistol and you'll lose your nuts." The man's eyes crossed as he was looking at the pistol touching his privates—his hands went straight up in the air. "Take it easy ma'am, please take your finger off the trigger and don't pull back the hammer."

"This is a double action pistol, and I don't have to pull back the hammer for it to fire. Want me to demonstrate?"

Max woke up the one on the ground, tied

his hands behind his back, with pigging strings, and did the same with the one looking at Sylvia's pistol.

While Sylvia was still selling produce, Max brought his two trouble makers to the jail. As he entered, no one was at the desk. Max yelled out, "anybody here?" Deputy Conover yelled back, "here, out back." Max walked out back and saw the deputy locked in his own jail cell.

"What is going on?" as he unlocked the cell door.

Sam explained, "once a week, several cowhands come to town from the Bar S ranch. Instead of getting their jollies at McElvey's saloon, they spend the day extorting money from the merchants. Last week they did the same thing and I went to the Bar S Ranch to talk to Mr. Scruggs. He laughed in my face and told me to get out. Today, these four arrogant ass holes, locked me up at gun point before they started their tirade on the merchants."

"Well, I've got two on horses for your jail." As they stepped outside the deputy asked what happened to one's face?

"He's some kind of idiot, he kept walking into our wagons."

After locking them up, Max asked, "how many others are there?"

"Two more, they'll hit every business in town and will hit the bank hard and last to bring their total up—then spend the night drinking the money away and laughing all the way back to the ranch."

"I see, I'll be back with two more."

Max went straight to the hardware store and found Floyd had already paid $4 for today's protection. Max ordered and paid for two very specific "items" and told Floyd he'd bring back his money. He then headed to the Merchants Bank. Stepping on the boardwalk he saw two men coming out of the mercantile and counting their collection. Max saw them walk across the street to the bank. As Max entered the bank, the president was looking out the window and knew what was coming. Max said to Mr. Bulow, "sir, go back to your office and I'll take care of those two."

Max stepped up to the teller and was preparing his daily deposit from the farmer's market. The two came swaggering in, pushed Max aside and told the teller to fork over $8 for today's protection service. Max stepped up to the man counting the money and said, "sir, it's illegal to extort money for protection. Give the money back or else!"

"Or else what?'

"Or, I will shoot you in the foot and take it away from you."

"Ha Ha Ha, you don't even have a gun! On second thought, give me your money also, or else."

From under his vest, Max's Bulldog came flying out and he shot the bully in the foot. All the tellers jumped, and Mr. Bulow came running out of his office, saying, "what on earth?" The bully was rolling on the floor and holding his boot with a clear hole in the boot top and the sole as well. He managed to get his boot off and kept holding his foot as he moaned and groaned. Max showed no pity, he pulled the cash out of the bully's pocket, as well as the one standing. He then said to the second bully, "unless you want the same treatment, you'd better get on the floor face down and put your hands in your back."

Both men were hog ticd with their hands in their backs and rolled onto their backs. Max then said, "you are both stupid animals to mistreat other humans like you did. Since 'I cannot fix stupid,' I can only persuade you to never patronize and humiliate another person. This should convince you," Max then took a bull-ring out of his pocket, opened it, and grabbed the man's nose with his left hand. Without hesitation, he shoved the pointed end of the ring into the man's nasal septum, closed it, and snapped it closed, as it automatically locked.

The screaming was delayed but very effective. The other bully turned white when Max took out a second bull-ring. During the ring's insertion, the man messed his pants and vomited all over himself. To emphasize what humiliation does to a man, Max tied a string to the rings and lead them to jail just like the animals they were.

The next day, Deputy Conover, said to Max, "I got a telegram from Judge Labby and he'll be here in a week. For the charge of extortion, these four will be in jail till the judge arrives. So, how do we remove the bull-rings before the judge gets here?"

"They are locked, so it takes an anvil, cold chisel and the strong arm of a blacksmith."

"Oh well, our blacksmith doesn't make house-calls."

"Since these cowhands will be here a week or possibly longer, someone has to notify their boss."

"Well, it won't be me, Scruggs is not only ornery, he's downright dangerous."

"Since I put them here, I'll go and give him the news."

Riding five miles west of town, Max arrived at the Bar-S Ranch. Out of courtesy, he rode up to the ranch house, and stayed on his horse as he yelled, "hello the house." An older, ill kept, white haired man, with a pot belly came to the door and said, "who are you and what do you want?"

"I'm the messenger. Your four cowhands that went to town a few days ago extorted money from the merchants for the second and last time. They are all in jail, will be there till the judge gets here, and will likely end up with months in the county prison. Better start looking for replacements. And by the way, two have bull-rings in their noses. So better send your blacksmith to cut them off. The town blacksmith doesn't make house-calls."

Max did not wait for an answer, he turned his horse and rode away. Scruggs yelled out, "when I find out who did this, he's going to pay dearly."

Max knew that he should keep riding, but it was beyond his control. He went back to the house and said, "I stopped all four and did a citizen's arrest. Since you treat an unruly bull with a bull-ring, I also treated two of the bullies with a bull-ring. Now, I'm an old bounty hunter and if you come after me or my family, I will end up killing you—that's a true-fact."

A week later, Judge Labby held the trial. There were several witnesses that confirmed the extortion by physical threat. Scruggs was the only witness for the defense. His claim was that this was all a mistake, and he would make financial restitution for payments made and loss of business. The jury did not buy the defense and came back with guilty verdicts. The judge sentenced all four to one year in the county prison.

The beginning of the second season started well. The new employees were quick learners and were happy to be gainfully employed. Sylvia was four months pregnant, and Jenna was already six months along. The new employees quickly filled in and the pregnant gals had plenty of rest periods.

Max had gone west of town to look for a new retail market. Finding a small town now fourteen miles from the homestead, meant a full day's travel to get to the farmer's market. Eggs, and some vegetables did not tolerate too much bumping around without cracking eggs or bruising soft vegetables. So, this new site would not be selling produce till the second day. The trip back would be on the second day.

Max reserved a spot in the farmer's market, set up an account at the local bank and was now advertising for two employees to take over the route. He had a sign at the bank, mercantile and hardware store. One day, to his surprise, Wilbur Haggerton, came to the homestead.

"Wonder if you remember me, Mr. Adams."

"I never forget someone who saves my butt. When I was hiring for the new set of workers, I wondered if you'd apply, but you never showed up. And, by the way, my name is Max."

"You were looking for full time help. With your financial donation, I've been able to make a living on the homestead, and I couldn't abandon the family and homestead. Now the young-ones are thinking of going to college in Laredo. They are old enough to take care of the farm a few days a week. This would free me a bit, and I could spend the two days doing your run. Also, my brother has the same financial need for secondary education and could handle the other wagon."

"You're both hired. I'll pay $5 each for the two-day run. All your over-night camping food and supplies are included. I expect you to be armed and make your sales deposit at the bank before heading back. If you have any left-over vegetables or eggs, stop at St. Helens Orphanage on the way home and empty your wagons."

With the makings of a properly organized new year, Max wondered what would happen to alter the planned course. He then realized that whatever happened, the business would manage and adjust. The real unknown, was looking down the road to childbirth, parenthood, and the ever present chance for revenge.

***

CHAPTER 14—Life's Moments

Meanwhile, in Mexico, Juan Guerra had experienced the worse year of his life. The Marlin nail had caused a hand infection which lead to losing two fingers to gangrene. His loss of teeth had been corrected by complete upper and lower false-teeth—requiring painful extractions of remaining teeth to form two partials. Worse of all, the amputated nose tip had healed with a pucker that made his nose look like a pig's snout.

For months, the Marquis had endured many topical treatments to change the nose's appearance—all to no benefit. The Marquis being of nobility and full of vanity, refused to go out of his office without a face mask. Seeing that this humiliation would never change, he agreed with his doctors to go to Houston Texas and have surgery to rebuild his nose.

During these horrible months, all the Marquis could think about was revenge against the American, Max Adams. Yet, the local police Captain had warned him against sending

Mexican Nationals across the border for a second time. If he was to attempt this again, with the border laws on the books, he would be arrested and imprisoned. That would be the ultimate insult and humiliation from his own people. This meant, that while in Houston, he would have to make contact with the most violent of outlaws to guarantee the death of Max Adams by Texans.

Before traveling to Houston, the Marquis' attorney found the name of the most ruthless outlaw with many men just as evil as it's leader, C J Horskins, known as the "Mutilator." Between the Mexican attorney and an American attorney, they were able to set up a meeting in Buford Texas between the Mutilator and the Marquis' Mexican attorney. A fee of $10,000 US was paid for Adams to be mutilated and living. If this was impossible, then death by torture. The event was to take place while the Marquis was recovering in the Houston hospital. The reconstructive operation was a two-step surgical approach some ten days apart. This gave the Mutilator some three weeks before the Marquis went back to Mexico.

The three saloons in town were always busy. The Wet Bucket offered liquor and meals.

McCloud's Tavern offered liquor and cards. McElvey's King of Spades offered meals, piano music, saloon girls, upstairs private services, liquor, house faro dealer, high stakes poker, and rooms to rent by the night. The first two served the local working class. The King of Spades took in anyone, had the most fights and shootings, and would operate daily from noon to 5AM.

McCelvey employed two bartenders. The first worked from noon to 8PM and the second took over at 8PM till 5AM. Both of these men were very capable and other than pouring drinks, they were the official bouncers—either wielding a bat or shotgun. Neil Bassett was the evening bar tender. He was also Sheriff Silvers friend and his source for the reporting of nefarious activity.

On his evening shift, patrons talked more since the liquor was loosening their tongues. Neil heard someone asking about a bounty hunter turned farmer. When the talk was that he came to town once a week at the farmer's market, and his farm was four miles east of town, the questions stopped. That same evening four men rented two rooms upstairs, for one week and paid in advance. The next day, Neil met with Wes at Kate's diner for lunch.

"Well, Wes, you've been back to work two weeks now, how do you feel?"

"I'm doing fine, and how are things at the King of Spades." "Well, funny you should ask, but something is brewing." After hearing the story, Wes decided he would visit the saloon tonight to try placing a face to wanted posters. In preparation for his evening walk-thru town, Wes went thru the wanted posters. He thought it was strange to find four posters in a row that had faces and writeups on the Mutilator's gang.

At the end of his walk-thru, he stepped thru McElvey's batwing doors and pulled up to the bar. He ordered a beer, and then turned his back to the bar. He immediately saw a table with the same four faces he had seen on the wanted posters. He finished his beer and went back to the office to confirm his finding—all four were wanted dead or alive. In the AM, Wes would go see Max and warn him.

Meanwhile, in an abandoned barn on the outskirts of town, a group of well-armed homesteaders had gathered. Their name was the BFR group (Benefactor Fund Recipients). Wilbur Haggerton called the meeting to order and asked Deputy Conover to bring the group up to date.

The deputy started, "one of McElvey's saloon girls, Suzie, was giving private service to one of the Mutilator's men. He was drunk and talked too much. He told her that he and his three partners were here to kill Max Adams." Wilbur asked, "is there any man here who doubts this information?" With no one speaking up, Wilbur said, "Max use to be one of the top bounty hunters and a true gunslinger. However, he has put aside the gun and taken to the plow. I happen to know that he no longer practices his draw. If we don't act soon, Max is dead, and his death will be on our shoulders. I say we collect these four, who are wanted dead or alive, hang them, and deposit the reward in his benefactor account." The vote to save Max was unanimous.

The next morning Wes rode to see Max at the farm. "It appears that the rumors are correct. We have four of C J Horskins' men at McElvey's saloon and they are here to kill you."

"Are they wanted dead or alive?"

"Yes."

"Then this is the perfect time to pick them up since they'll all be sleeping off a big drunk. Let me get my pistol and I'll help you get them into your jail."

Arriving in town, they stopped at the jail to pickup Deputy Conover. Stepping off their horse, there was a lot of activity around the undertaker's parlor. Wes asks, "what's all that hubbub at the undertaker. Well last night, those four of Horskins' gang were hung by the vigilante group, the BFR's.

Max asked, "who are they?"

Wes added, don't you know, 'the Benefactor Fund Recipients,' lead by Wilbur Haggerton."

A flash went on in Max's head. "Oh no. I need to talk with Wilbur. This vigilante activity must stop."

Later, Wilbur came to the sheriff's office to meet with Wes and Max. On arrival, Wilbur asked that the reward money be directly deposited into the Benefactor account. Max looked surprised and asked? "is that why you hung those four?"

"No, we hung them because they were going to kill you. You are out of practice with the gun, and they would have gunned you down. We couldn't let that happen. It wasn't for us to collect the money. It so happens that good people may benefit from it in the long run, heh."

Wes looked at Max and said, "they have a good point."

Max explained. "Let's forget last night's hanging. Look in the future. Horskins will come back since I know who is paying him. The next time, I want Wes, Sam, Sylvia and myself to take care of them. I need your word on this."

"As long as you don't take them on by yourself. And give the Missus a sawed-off double barrel shotgun to even the odds."

Max thought about the well know bounty hunters, Wayne Swanson and Cal Harnell, who had both use sawed-off shotguns carried on a holster tied to their backs. He pictured Sylvia with such a contraption and so he went directly to McClellan's gun shop. When he explained that he was looking for a modified shotgun for Sylvia to handle, Omer said he had the right thing. He took out a double 12 gauge with two triggers and two external hammers called 'mule ears." He also had in stock, a back holster that was held by adjustable universal straps. He told Max to go to Kate's diner for breakfast, run some errands, and the shotgun would be cut down, the trigger-pull lightened, and the opening hinge loosened up—ready for a lady to handle.

Meanwhile, in San Antonio, the Mutilator was given the message that his four men were dead—hung by a vigilante group after his men had passed out from drinking. He had been in a rage all day and was drinking heavily. By evening, he met with his four other gang members. "Guess, if you want a job done right, you've got to do it yourself. Now you four are my best men. We are going to that Valley town, and when we get there, we will do the job first, and celebrate after. Not the other way around like our four idiots did. We are well paid. I'll give you four men $5000 to split amongst yourselves—after the job is done. Any questions? Good, we leave on the morning train to Laredo and then take the ferry to the Valley town. According to the attorney for Mr. Guerra, that will put us in that town the afternoon that the target is in town on business and goes to the bank at

the end of the day. We'll be there
waiting for him."

"How do you know all this, boss?

"That attorney has a snitch in one of the Valley saloons."

Arriving home, Max explained to Sylvia what had happened. He also told her that the Marquis would likely send the Mutilator and more men the second time around. Sylvia spoke up, "you aren't going to go up against these men, alone are you?

"No, I'm going to need help from Wes and Sam."

"And me. You aren't going into a gunfight without me. I've spent all my life waiting for you, and I'm not taking any chance of losing you."

"But Sylvia, you are carrying our child."

"So what, pregnancy doesn't make a woman a zombie. I can still handle a gun and……. Max held up a hand, and handed her a box. She stopped talking, opened up the box, and pulled a smile from ear to ear. Max added, "I'd be happy to have you at my side."

The next week was uneventful on the farm.

Grant and Brian heard about the hanging and argued that they should handle the farmer's market in town. Both Max and Sylvia wouldn't allow it. When it came time, they loaded two wagons, and as they were preparing to leave, Wilbur shows up with a third wagon full of produce. "Don't shoot the messenger, Mr. Cassidy insisted that you have a rifle backup."

"Actually, that's a very good idea," said Sylvia.

The market was very busy, and the three workers ran around all day. They sold out by 3PM and walked to the Merchant's Bank to deposit their cash box. Wilbur was carrying his Win 73, Max had his pistol and Sylvia had her sawed-off shotgun in her back holster as well as her Bull Dog on her side—with a small pregnant paunch to match.

Before entering the bank, Max stopped, as he realized that he had not set up any rules of engagement. He said "assuming there are five shooters in front of us, Sylvia, you take on the two on the left, Wilbur you take the middle man, and I'll take the two on the right. If there are more, it's anyone's game, but remember Sylvia only has two shots. Also, to mislead them, Wilbur stay on the sideline as if you're not in the fight. They'll think they have an advantage. It's all about the psychology of gunfighting."

Walking in the bank, Wilbur spotted chairs and several folks sitting on the bank's boardwalk. He sat down and covered his rifle with a newspaper. When Max and Sylvia were finished their business, they turned around and saw five men standing in the middle of the street. "The second from the right is Horskins, and he's all mine." Sylvia pulled out her shotgun and cocked both hammers back. "Ok, let's put an end to this threat and move on with our lives."

***

Max followed Sylvia out on the boardwalk and nodded to Wilbur who already, had the newspaper off his rifle, and had the hammer pulled back. Yet Wilbur stayed sitting down. As Sylvia stepped down, she moved a bit to the left, as Max went a bit to the right. This gave Wilbur a clear shot at the middle man. Sylvia held her shotgun above her hip ready to fire at the man on the far left, then move to the number four man. Max made the decision to go for the number two man first—the mutilator. He was likely the fastest draw, then move to number one and then look for standing stragglers.

With the hammer loop off, Max asked, "are you looking for me?"

"If you're Max Adams we are. I was given two choices to deal with you, but now I'm choosing a third option."

"What were the choices the Marquis gave you?"

"To mutilate you but let you live or torture you to death. Now I'm so angry with what happened to my men, that I've decided to outright shoot you down as well as your wife and your unborn child. That will be the Marquis' revenge. Then I'm going to hunt down every member of the BFR vigilante group and hang each one."

"You might reconsider this gunfight, my wife has a scattergun, loaded with OO Buckshot, which will even the odds."

"The way we look at it, a pregnant woman won't know what to do once the shooting starts—ha,ha,ha."

"Suit yourselves, it's your funeral."

Horskins hesitated, looked to the sides and backwards, to assure he had not missed a rear or flank gun. "I'm sure. Get ready boys."

"Remember, your nemesis is looking you in the eye." A phrase that alerted Sylvia and Wilbur. Suddenly, Horskins eyes closed for a few seconds—signaling his brain was commencing his draw. Horskins yelled, "now" and all five went for their pistols. Five shots immediately rang out, the street was full of black acrid smoke, and five outlaws were in different stages of collapsing, when a late shot rang out. One of the outlaws (number one) held his pistol pointing at the ground and in the last throws of life, his trigger finger spasmed and fired at the ground. Sylvia saw a large spark as the bullet hit the ground and at the same time heard Max yelp and groan as he collapsed to the ground.

Max was stunned but was able to relate to Sylvia, "that was a ricochet that hit me, I see that I have a piece of my front shirt missing. do I have an exit wound in the back?"

Sylvia rolled him and looked. "No."

"Good God, that's worse, get me to Doc Murphy," as he passed out."

Sylvia yelled for some help as townspeople started to approach. A wagon and driver arrived next to Max and Sylvia asked if he would take

Max to the hospital. The townspeople loaded Max on the wagon bed and Sylvia sat next to Max. Within minutes, they arrived at the new hospital receiving area. Doc Murphy was standing in the doorway with his wife.

Doc Murphy said, "we knew from the extensive shooting that the wounded would be coming here, so who are you bringing Sylvia?"

"It's Max, he has a ricochet hit to the right chest without an exit wound and a piece of his shirt missing."

Doc Murphy was shocked to see Max unconscious and having a sucking sound to his breathing. They transferred Max to a gurney and wheeled him into the hospital. Doc Murphy pushed the gurney into the operating room and his wife closed the doors. Mrs. Murphy told Sylvia that one of them would give them more info as soon as possible.

A full hour passed, and Wes had joined Sylvia. They were both waiting for some news as Doc Murphy came out. "I'm going to give you the facts, and don't ask questions—there's no time. Max has a bullet in his lung with a piece of his shirt. This bullet and the detritus must be removed, or he will die. On top of it all, he has a collapsed lung and he is bleeding in his chest. I have to operate, and it's a complicated procedure, so I'll do my best and pray for us." Doc Murphy turned around and walked back to the operating room. Sylvia turned to Wes and broke into a heart wrenching cry.

Meanwhile in the operating room, The Doc's wife was ready to administer drop ether at the Doc's command. A rubber tube was inserted in the chest's upper side to a water bottle that would trap air and help inflate the lung. A second rubber tube in his lower chest was to drain blood. During the procedure, Max started to awaken, and drop ether was started to keep him under a light anesthetic. The Doc then inserted a forcep thru the bullet hole and failed to make contact with the bullet. He then decided to extend the bullet hole and insert a rib separator. With a special gas lamp overhead, Doc saw the hole in the lung, inserted the forcep and said, "I can feel the bullet and here it comes. He and the Missus could see a deformed bullet with a large piece of shirt material. His wife removed the detritus and applied it to the shirt on the table—it was a perfect fit. The last thing the Doc did was add a powder in the lung and closed the wound after sterilizing the edges for the second time. Once the air trapping bottle stopped bubbling and the blood bottle was getting drainage at a trickle, Doc Murphy realized that Max might survive. The last thing Doc Murphy did was to start an intravenous line and run in slowly a bottle of sterile salt water with sugar. This was a new experimental treatment to maintain nutrition and hydration. Now, he had to explain all this to the crowd in the waiting room.

Doc Murphy entered and the waiting room was packed. He recognized" Grant and Nellie, Brian and Jenna, Elbert and Bess, Wes and Meg,

G. Sweeney and Wilbur, Merchants Bulow-Thabo-Kate-Stevenson-Emerson-Caldwell-Sammy Craven. He then asked Sylvia in private, "He is stable and if we are lucky, he will survive. Do you want me to give you the facts in private or do you want me to share everything with the waiting room?"

"You told me what I wanted to hear. Now, these are his family and friends. They need to know everything."

Doc Murphy started explaining everything that he had done to Max, especially the operation, and what the function of the tubes were. Not realizing its significance, he asked if there were any questions. The onslaught began: "What are his chances for survival?" "What is this powder you left in his chest?" "What are the chances for infection?" "Can we see him?"

"As far as survival, before these modern surgical approaches, this kind of gunshot was universally fatal. I firmly believe that Max has a high likelihood of surviving. The powder I left in his chest was a powder that promotes blood to congeal and stop the lung from bleeding. Later it will dissolve and disappear. As far as infection, my surgical instruments were soaking in carbolic acid, I scrubbed my hands and forearms with a brush and lye soap. Before the operation I rinsed my hands in carbolic acid as well as Max's chest and wound. It's hoped that this will prevent infection from these "germs" that are not visible."

With an apparent exhaustion of questions, Doc Murphy added, "now we have an open policy of visiting hours as long as you are not ill. Sylvia will stay with him continuously and will sleep on a cot in the room. You may all go in, two at a time, to see him while he's still under anesthesia—but for 5 minutes or less. Starting tomorrow, you may stay 10 minutes at a time. Remember those tubes and bottles are what will likely save his life. If everything goes well in a few days, you'll be able to visit until Sylvia mentions its Max's nap time. That will be your cue that it's time to leave."

Everyone entered for minutes to see that Max was breathing and attached to a fanatic array of bottles and tubes. Upon leaving, Nellie went to Kate's Diner and arranged for a meal to be sent to Sylvia three times a day, and add Max to the schedule when authorized by the Doc.

Eventually, Sylvia sat by Max's bed and was determined to stay by his side till he awoke from anesthesia. Four hours passed when Max opened his eyes to see Sylvia sitting next to his bed.

Sylvia stood, bent over and kissed her husband on the lips. "Welcome back to the living, and don't ever scare me like that again!"

"What happened, where am I, and what are all these tubes coming out of my chest and my arm?"

After Sylvia gave him a simplified version of today's event, Max said, "but dear, a ricochet gunshot is a fatal wound!"

"Not any more with Doc Murphy involved, with modern equipment and surgical technique, and of course a modern hospital from an anonymous donation—I wonder where that money came from?"

"Oh yes, I'm beginning to remember." As Max fell back asleep.

The next week proved to be a day by day event. During the first day postop Max slept most of the time because of the morphine dosing. He would awaken every two hours, take some water and talk to Sylvia a few minutes. Doc Murphy came to check him every two hours, and his wife was in and out continuously.

The second day is when the air bubbling

stopped, and the blood bottle didn't have any new collections. The doctor was a bit worried about a low grade-fever for the past two days but attributed it to tissue reaction from trauma. With less morphine on board, Max was awake 50% of the time. Sylvia explained what the doctor was finding on his exams and what was the significance of the bottle changes. The tube in his hand delivering experimental fluids was pulled since Max was taking a full liquid diet to include puddings and oatmeal.

Meanwhile in Houston, the Marquis had been given the bad news about the demise of the Mutilator's nine men. Four at the hands of the BFR and five at the hands of Max, wife and friend. He was furious. He asked his new segundo, "is there not one man on this earth that can kill that couple?" The segundo answered, "I have already checked with our American attorney and he has given me the name of an accomplished assassin that has never fouled up his assignment. He goes by the name 'the exterminator' and is available for a fee of $5,000, paid in advance."

"Ah yes, in this country, everything is paid in advance. There is no honor amongst thieves and murderers as we have in our country. Very well, pay him but I want it done this week while he's still in the hospital and is vulnerable."

The third day was a test day. The rubber tubes were clamped for two hours. At the end, the clamps were removed, and the bottles stayed inactive. The test was repeated for six hours with the same results. Doc Murphy was pleased, especially with the low-grade fever resolved. The most reassuring clinical finding was the full expanding and contracting of the damaged lung. Max was occasionally sitting up in a chair and taking regular meals and plenty of fluids.

On this morning, Wilbur was heading a meeting in the abandoned barn. "It's clear that Max will live. He is at significant risk while recovering in the hospital and this is where we can come in as a group.

> We have an attendance of 26 BFR members—and that is 100% of the group. I propose that we use five members on each eight-hour shift and provide two men at the front and rear door as well as one man at Max's hospital door. This is the least we can do until he returns home. The goal is to detain any stranger appearing at the hospital doors." With total support, people signed up to keep the schedule manned at all times.

The fourth day, the tubes came out. Doc Murphy didn't want the tubes to be a source of a late infection. Max was eating full meals brought in by Kate's Diner and was beginning to walk in the room. As bodily functions returned, the call of nature took over. When Max asked Sylvia to help him to the water closet, she pulled a commode next to the bed and motioned at him to use it. "Doesn't each room have a water closet?"

"No, it has a sink to wash up with running hot and cold water, but no water closet. Maybe that anonymous donor can rectify this situation"—with a smile

"That's strange, I thought I had taken care of that, and how did you find out about my donation?"

"After we were married, you added my name to the account. When Wes brought me the outlaw's reward money, I deposited the Western Union vouchers into the Benefactor Fund. Looking at the account, Elmer Stevenson's withdrawals were all under $100. One withdrawal in the several thousand was paid to Doc Murphy. Thanks to your thinking in the future, you're probably alive because of Doc Murphy's medical advances."

"And remind me to take care of this water closet problem in the future. In addition, being a patient has given me the idea of which changes would be beneficial.

The fifth day, Max was beginning to think clearly. He started thinking of their security. He looked at Sylvia and said, "you've been wearing your Bull Dog on your hip since I woke up. What do you know about our security that I've missed?"

"The BFR has provided five armed men around the clock since yesterday morning. Wilbur told me they will stay on guard till we go home."

Sylvia knew Max was coming around when he asked for his Bull Dog and his belt holster. Sylvia was happy to oblige with the added security in the room. By the seventh day postop, Max was able to enjoy visiting with family and friends. Grant brought up the subject of long- term security. Max quickly responded.

"There's three ways to look at this problem. First there has to be a snitch that is passing info to Laredo's telegraph, about my comings and goings. That snake's head has to be cut off. The second, is eliminating an assassination attempt while I'm here in the hospital. The third is cutting off the dragon's head. Wes will take care of the first, the BFR or us will take care of the second, and I will take care of the dragon, myself."

"What about security at the farm?"

"If we take care of the three issues, we should be able to all live in piece in our homestead."

Max and Wes met and set up a sting. "McElvey, like the other saloons, place their orders via Gary Sweeney every week he travels to Laredo. I'm suspecting that McElvey's order has more than an order in his envelope. Talk to Gary and open his envelope. If there is a message plus his order, confiscate the extra note and add this one instead. This one says that the eliminator was successful."

After discussing the sting with the local judge, it was decided that as long as they didn't alter the saloon's order, that it was acceptable to alter the note with criminal intent. It would also prove that McElvey was the outlaw snitch.

Days passed and Max got stronger. He started walking in the hospital hallway and even started to walk outside, with the doorway guard at his side. Now, at the end of two weeks, Max was strong enough, and would be heading home in the morning. With no assassination attempt in ten days, everyone was beginning to relax.

Wilbur knew better. The second shift bartender, Neil, had heard a patron talk to locals about Max. The local homesteader mentioned that Max was in the Murphy Valley Hospital and would be going home soon. On this last night in the hospital, Wilbur was the doorway guard.

The evening was quiet, and Sylvia and Max fell soundly asleep. In the middle of the night, Wilbur felt sleepy, and stepped next to a heating stove to get a fresh cup of coffee. At the same time, a man wearing moccasins, stepped to the back entrance and found one guard asleep and the other walking to the privy. He quickly made his entry.

Walking thru the hospital patient rooms, only

one door was locked. The assassin used a strange tool and silently unlocked the door. As he entered, he knew he was in the right room, seeing a woman laying asleep on a cot. The assassin pulled out his knife and lifted up both hands in preparation to strike Max. Max heard a noise and woke up to hear the man say, "this is from the Marquis!"

At that instant, a shotgun blast was heard as the assassin's hands were blown off and the assassin was left in a state of shock, looking and trying to hold the two stubs where his hands use to be. Wilbur stepped forward, dropped the shotgun's barrel on the assassin's head, and knocked him out. He quickly tied pigging strings to his wrists to stop the bleeding. The other four guards quickly showed up and all five dragged the assassin out of the room. Max and Sylvia were also in a state of shock as they saw tissues, bones and fingers stuck on the room's west wall.

The assassin was brought to McElvey's saloon. He was gagged and a noose was put around his neck. Wilbur said, "we're going to hang you here, so the snitch can send the message back to the Marquis.

Before he was strung up from a porch beam, Wilbur checked the assassin's money belt and found $5,000. The assassin was groaning so loud that the lights came on in McElvey's upstairs bedroom. By the time he came downstairs to open the door, the assassin was violently struggling and kicking at the end of a rope, and his bowel and bladder had emptied themselves on McElvey's porch. Seeing the two stubs for hands, McElvey added to the excrements and vomited on the spot.

The next day, McElvey sent a double note to Laredo thru Gary Sweeney. Wes and Gary proceeded as planned. Opening McElvey's envelope, the note addressed to #419 (a code) was opened and they found the words, "the eliminator failed and was hung." Max's note was substituted with the same code #419. The judge then issued an arrest warrant. Wes decided to hold off arresting McElvey till the new note would get to the Marquis and further attempts on Max's life would stop. Then, he would be thrown in jail, to await trial for conspiracy to commit murder.

By morning Max and Sylvia had breakfast with Wilbur. "Well, Wilbur, this is the third time you save my life, what do I owe you?"

"I still owe you for saving my homestead and my pride. Oh, and here is $5,000 found in the assassin's pocket—blood money I'm sure.

Now, I'm going to get the buggy, take you both home, and get to work before your dad docks my pay for being late, heh!"

Waiting for Wilbur, Doc Murphy came to give his strong recommendation that Max needed a month's rest before going back to work. Max thanked him for saving his life and then asked, "what do I owe you for your services?"

"My regular fee is $20 for major surgery. The hospital charges include $5 for the operating room, $4 per day for room and board, $5 for chest tubes, bottles and vein fluids. $3 for morphine and laudanum, and $2 for cleaning fingers off the wall."

Sylvia was taking notes and said, "for +- two weeks, that roughly comes up to $86."

"That may be so, but your charge is zero. I'm so proud to have been able to save you with this investment of yours."

Sylvia looked at Max and shrugged her shoulder. "Well Doc, you may not charge me, but I can tip you for your services." As Max pulls out five one hundred US dollars."

"Well, this is an unexpected windfall, I certainly can use it to buy more supplies. Thank you again Max."

"Speaking of supplies and changes, here is a list

of things you need to add. I want you to get Mr. Thabo to build you a 'porte cochere' over your receiving entrance to the operating, a water closet in every patient room, and a kitchen. Hire a cook to provide patient meals and meals for you and your wife. Speaking of help, don't you think it's time for you and your wife to have help. You need a partner and your wife needs a nurse. So, start looking for a new doc out of training—maybe with a wife who is a nurse? This means, build them a house at the other end of the hospital. Attach it to the hospital like yours—or you take the new one and give the old one to the new doc, heh!"

"Stop—stop please. I cannot afford this. It would cost several thousand dollars."

"Nonsense, here is $4,500, the balance of the $5,000 in the assassin's pocket. Money he was paid to kill me. There is more if you need it. We were paid $6,000 for the mutilator's gang and we'll collect a reward of $2,000 for the assassin. It's all blood money, and the best place for it is in my benefactor fund or this hospital—for some good to come from it."

Doc Murphy stood there, confused and speechless. His wife stepped up, accepted the $4,500 and said, "my husband is very dedicated, and he respectfully accepts your donation. He wants all these changes and not one penny will be wasted. Thank You."

Wilbur arrived with the buggy as Wes arrived on a run. "I know you're heading home, but the Judge is holding McElvey's trial at noon today. The prosecutor is not planning on calling you as a witness, but the defense lawyer may. If you're not here, the trial will be delayed a week till the judge returns."

"Ok, I'll stay here and take a nap and an early lunch. I'll be at the trial. Wilbur you have the morning off till the trial starts.

The trial was the most confrontational and accusatory event of the year. The defense attorney claimed his client had been entrapped and his rights to privacy violated. The prosecutor admitted that a personal message had been tampered with but pointed out that this was not an opened postal envelope—and no crime had been committed. The judge pounded his mallet on and off to regain order between the prosecutor and the defense attorney. It was Sheriff Handy from Laredo who found the link man that transferred messages from McElvey to the Marquis. A letter confessing his activity tied McElvey to the Mutilator's gang.

In the end the prosecutor charged McElvey with two counts of conspiring to commit murder—once with the mutilator's gang and once with the assassin. Despite the heated proceedings, the jury came back in fifteen minutes with a guilty verdict on both counts. The judge immediately pronounced sentence. Ten years on each count, without a chance of parole. Being in his early 60's, this sentence was a death sentence. By law, the defendant's business would be sold thru the court and the funds returned to the town if no legal heirs claimed the assets.

Sylvia was a bit surprised at the heavy sentence. Max added, "I'm not, a man like McElvey follows certain patterns. He had a habit of beating his saloon girls which progressed to beating his wife. I was able to save his wife from his clutch, and he took his revenge against me by helping others to kill you and me. Justice has been served."

After coming to the end of a traumatic ordeal, Max was on his way home to recover and mount a final resolution to an unrelenting foe.

***

CHAPTER 15—Final Days

Recovering from major blood loss with shock and oxygen deprivation was a slow process. Although Max was able to walk on the town boardwalks and streets, walking in the fields was another matter. Max didn't have enough stamina to drive horses and maneuver the implement's handles and dials. He needed to stay out of the field for weeks. Instead of pushing himself beyond reason, he joined Sylvia in the greenhouse and helped with the glass tube seeding, watering, potting soil prep, and transplanting to clay pots.

With Nellie and Jenna's help, the four of them planted 4,000 glass tubes and transplanted 1,000 tube plants to clay pots. The newest addition to winter crops, started in the greenhouse, was a trial of Jalapeno peppers. The demand was there and so the producers responded accordingly.

During the greenhouse plantings, Max and Sylvia used their time to discuss some issues. "I know something has to be done about the Marquis, since it's just a matter of time before he finds out we're alive and engineers another attempt on our lives. What do you think we should do?"

"Either we convince him to abandon this idea of revenge, and move on with his life, or we have to kill him."

"How can we accomplish the former?"

"By asking for a peaceful truce, by threatening to harm his family and heirs, by torturing him, or by having him shanghaied to a slow ship around the world."

"Well let's analyze these four options. First, you can't have a peaceful truce with a rattlesnake. Second, he has no family or heirs. Third, we've already cut off his nose, nailed him to his desk and forced back two fingers and it didn't work. Last, if shanghaied, he will eventually return and will be so furious that he'll send a small army to eliminate us and our families. Any more choices? How about the law in Mexico or the US?"

"The law in either country can discuss it with him, but unless there is proof of his direct involvement, nothing will change."

"Sylvia, there's only one more choice, we have to kill him."

"I never thought I would agree to a plot like this, but you're right. He is now in the US. If we kill him here, we'll likely be arrested for his murder."

"You're right, we have to do this in Mexico, thru an anonymous assassination."

"I suspect he's quite comfortable in Houston and will stay there indefinitely when he finds out we're alive. How do we get him booted out of the country?"

"Funny you should ask. Wes and I have already been working on this. Our prosecutor has filed charges in our county and requested extraditing the Marquis to our county. It has failed but the local authorities have been questioning a well-known shady attorney. In return for keeping his law license, he has agreed to implicate the Marquis in hiring the Horskins gang and the Eliminator to kill me. With any luck, the Marquis will be heading back to Mexico. The Mexican officials had to apologize to US officials for the Marquis' behavior. He will be deported to his home-town as a 'persona non grata.'"

"Ok, well it looks like you're ahead of me on this one. Normally, I would insist on going with you, but there is a complication. Yesterday I had a checkup with Doc Murphy. I have been having low back aches for two weeks. I thought it was because of my sitting at your bedside for long periods of time. The doctor told me it is because of the baby changing my posture. He is recommending a walk twice a day and only short trips on horseback—such as riding to town and back the same day.

He does not want me to take long riding trips as is required to get to the Marquis in Mexico."

"I understand, this is my responsibility and I shall do it alone."

"Do you think the Mexican authorities will come after you?"

"No. His death would be a blessing in disguise. He is now a national embarrassment. Were he to die without heirs, his properties and assets would be confiscated by the government. The proceeds would be returned to the community or the county."

"Do you have any qualms about doing this?"

"Remember the old Bounty Hunter saying, 'I do not risk my life to try saving the life of a killer!' Well, I will kill anyone who risks my life or the life of my loved ones. It's self-defense and self-preservation."

"Well, I realize that this is our responsibility, but in my absence, I will find you a backup.

You are not going on a two-day journey alone. I know I can find one man out of 26 benefactor recipients."

The next day, Sylvia had a private meeting with the known BFR leader, Wilbur Haggerton. After explaining the situation, Sylvia asked if she could hire a man to assist Max as his backup. Wilbur answered, "this could take up to ten days to completion if the Marquis only comes out of his home but once a week to visit his lady friend. The BFR group are all homesteaders who cannot leave the work for so long. As is my case, I would prefer that I be his backup, but my children are harvesting our hay crop, and I have to help them every day when I finish my shift here on your farm."

"Let me make you an offer you can't refuse. I'll double your pay during these ten days and will send men to help your children. When you return, your hay crops will all be in the barn."

"Wow, what a deal. I'm honored to be at your husband's side."

When Max was told who his backup would be, he was more than pleased. He then met with Wilbur and told him he would need to shoot a long-range scoped rifle at 600 yards to serve as his backup. Every day, for the next two weeks, Max and Wilbur took the time, out of their work schedules, to practice long range shooting from 300-600 yards.

The rifle used was a Win 1876. It shot a 350-grain bullet at 1500 feet per second. A board 18 in. wide by 6 feet high was placed at the four yardages—three, four, five and six hundred yards. Max explained. "This bullet will travel five hundred yards, or fifteen hundred feet, in one second. Whereas, the sound will take three seconds to get to the target. The smoke bloom will appear instantaneously before the bullet reaches its target."

Wilbur asked, "what is our goal with these guns."

"We need to hit our target within a four-inch circle at 200-300 yards, and an eight-inch circle at 400-600 yards. That means, we both need to practice till proficient. Hopefully, we will both do the shooting, but if either is incapacitated, the other man would need to take the shot."

Day after day, they would meet two hours before the end of Wilbur's shift. At first, hitting a standardizing 18-inch square target at 200 yards became their baseline. Adjusting the Malcolm scope to move up to 300 yards was a learning experience. All shooting was on a tripod rest. The 300-yard target was easily mastered with a tight 4-inch pattern. The 400-yard target adjustment on the scope were recorded to be committed to memory—as well as the 500 and 600-yards setting.

It took a week to move beyond 500 yards to the maximum yardage of six hundred yards. Even thru an 8X power, that man size target was getting very small. Since the ultimate target was expected to be either 500 or 600 yards away, the shooters needed to master either settings or anything in-between. It was clear that the rifling was capable of keeping the bullets in an eight-inch circle at 600 yards. Any variation beyond eight inches was the shooter's fault. Getting use to the tripod for stability was of utmost importance.

After days of practice and more practice, Max and Wilbur began to raise hell with that eight-inch circle on the target's upper half—being center mass on a man's chest. Having reached their goal, Max suggested they take a few days off and then return to the range. If they could maintain their accuracy on their first shot, they would pass the test and be ready.

During Max's days off, he rode east looking to find local cattle ranches that had large piles of old composted horse manure. He arranged on purchasing 'mega loads' for 75 cents each. Although most homesteaders used their own chicken manure in their gardens, Max was lucky to find a chicken farm that raised chickens for the meat. They had a huge pile of composted manure that they sold for 50 cents per each "mega load." The extra miles were offset by the low cost and almost an endless supply. Max was quite sure that two men could get to the chicken farm, load the spreader extra full, drive the load back to the farm and spread it before the end of the work day. With the local horse manure, the same two men could make two loads a day.

For the last thing on his agenda, he continued east and found a medium size settlement, yet unnamed, and arranged for a site at the farmer's market. His cost for the year was $25 and payable in advance to the local bank. While at the bank, he opened an account for the business. That allowed for the sales person to make a deposit at the bank, and not carry large amounts of cash on the trail back home. This retail site would require camping out overnight since this was a two- day event.

Having finished his business, he returned home. Picking up Wilbur they went for their proficiency exam. In attendance were Grant, Nellie, Jenna and Sylvia. The requirement for passing the exam was placing a bullet, six hundred yards downrange, in an eight-inch circle followed by a follow-up shot within five seconds—also in the same eight-inch circle.

Wilbur stepped up, took his time for his first shot and took his second shot within four seconds. Max took his turn and duplicated the process, but his second shot was within three seconds. A rider went down to get the targets but came back with only one. When asked why he didn't bring the other target, he answered, "no need to, the two holes were the same as this one"—showing two holes in center mass within an eight-inch circle. Sylvia looked at Max and said, "you guys are ready, just come back alive."

***

The next day, Max and Wilbur went to town to pick up supplies for the trail. While Wilbur picked up the food supplies, Max went to the hardware store for special items, and then went to the hospital to pick up another special item from Doc Murphy. Early the next morning, Sylvia awoke Max with passionate kisses. She then said, "during my visit with Doc Murphy, I asked him if it was Ok to resume marital activity. He said yes."

"That's good since you've got me halfway there already." Afterwards, Sylvia added, "there's more of that in the future, but you have to come back to me?"

After a hearty breakfast, Wilbur and Max took off on their mission. Instead of using a packhorse, they elected to use two extra-large saddlebags for each horse. This allowed for greater traveling speed. Each horse had two scabbards, one for the Win 73 and one for the Win 76. With fresh horses, they rode south for a solid two hours before resting and watering their horses. They continued this routine, but at lunch, the horses were allowed to crop some lush grass. They rode till dark and estimated they had covered some forty miles—more than half the way to the Marquis' ranch.

After tethering the horses next to forage and water, Max set up camp as Wilbur started the fire. This would be their only hot meal till their return home. Wilbur had chosen precooked foods that would stay fresh for one week. In addition, tonight they would cook all the extra meats and bake a one-week supply of biscuits. After a good night's sleep and a breakfast of coffee, bacon and beans, they resumed riding.

They had only been on the road for two hours when they came onto a campsite. Max took a good look and thought he recognized the man. Getting closer, the man walked toward them. Max recognized him and explained to Wilbur who the unarmed man was. "This is one of the segundo's men who was sent to ambush me. Because he was not armed, I only killed his partner who shot at me. I gave him a shotgun, a box of 00 Buckshot and $50—and here he is again."

"Yes senor, my name is Antonio Ramirez, and this is my wife Juanita, who is with child. Juanita has just cooked some breakfast burritos and we would like you to join us. I have a story to tell you."

Max looked at Wilbur and said, "Why not, I suspect we will learn something of value." After tethering their horses next to the stream with good grasses, they joined their hosts. Wilbur was introduced and they sat down to share some coffee and burritos. Once done with the snack, Antonio started his story.

"Years ago, my young mother was a maid in Marquis Guerra's hacienda. One night he raped my mother repeatedly. The next morning, she escaped to her parents' home. She later discovered she was pregnant. Her father made a report to the local policia who at least made a formal report to the judicial bureau—nothing was done to the important Marquis. The baby was born, and its mother worked as a cleaning lady and waitress to support herself and her child. That child was me, as you might suspect."

"Later in life, I found out thru my mother, that the Marquis Guerra was my biological father. After years of denying my existence and refusing to help my mother financially, I elected to find out more on the subject and anonymously I took employ on the ranch. Later, my attorney filed an injunction against the Marquis. A hearing was held, and the Marquis didn't show up, only his aggressive attorney."

"The witness was my elderly mother and the complaint filed in the judicial bureau decades earlier. The Marquis's attorney used every vile word possible to imply that my mother was a whore. Several of the town's people were called to uphold my mother's character. The result was a judge's order to legally list me as an heir and to add my name to his will. Until his death, nothing will change, but once he passes, I will become the new owner of his hacienda, cattle and land. In addition, my mother will move into the guest quarters, permanently."

"I see, and I surmise you know what we are doing here."

"Yes senor. The entire community knows, and we all know it is in our community's best interest. Since his first failure to abduct your wife, he has become cruel to his household helpers, cowhands and even the local merchants. He has become an evil vindictive man. In addition, since his expulsion from the US, he has also lost face with the Mexican authorities. Consequently, he rarely comes out of his hacienda, on business or pleasure, like he use to. He will be hard to kill with all the security around him, day and night."

"Interesting. Something tells me we will meet again. Thank you for the information and warning. I assume you'll return to your home now that we met."

"Yes, my mission is complete, and we will

return to our home with my mother, to await the birth of our first child. Good hunting. I'm returning the shotgun you gave me, which is also the reason I gave my mother for our trip to intercept you, heh."

"Keep it, one day I hope to see it over your fireplace, as a reminder of the right decision I made years ago." Antonio nodded and Juanita smiled.

The duo rode hard all day and were able to make it to within a few miles of the hacienda. With time to spare, they found an outcropping of large trees some 500+ yards to the hacienda. Setting back a half mile, they set up a cold camp with a spring nearby and good grass—a spot where their horses could be tethered all day.

That night they had cold roast beef sandwiches, cold coffee and cookies. In the AM they had cold coffee, biscuits and cheese. They then collected what they needed for the day. Two rifles, two tripods, a 50X Binocular with tripod, canteens with water, cheese, crackers, cold bacon and jerky. In case of sunlight, they had leather antireflective hoods for the scopes and binoculars.

They chose their observation and shooting

spot carefully. It was situated at the edge of a forest outcropping of leafless trees but with chest high bushes for camouflage. The leafless hardwood trees allowed enough daylight to brighten the scope's and binoculars' view. They set up all three tripods and focused the binoculars on the hacienda. The rifle tripods were set to place the scopes on the front door.

Once set up, they started their surveillance. They were watching the general activity around the house, yard and barns. Their major point of interest was the carriage house attached to the barn. If the carriage was harnessed, that would be a sign the Marquis would be coming out to step in his ride. Every half hour, the observers rotated on the binoculars. By dark, no useful pattern of activity was detected, and no visitors arrived on the scene.

Back at their cold camp with all the surveillance gear. Max said, "I strongly believe that Antonio was on the money. This scoundrel will eventually order his next assassination without ever coming out of his hole. I think we need to force him out with an injury needing medical attention."

"Why wouldn't he just send for the local doctor?"

"Because he has become 'persona non grata' and the local doctor has already been chastised for a poor nasal reconstruction. No, I believe he will have to seek and travel to an outside medical facility."

"Ok, how do we accomplish this?"

"This is what we're going to do. I have a bottle of chloroform. Sneaking up on the two sleeping guards, you will hold a pistol to the guard's head. I will pour the chloroform on a towel and apply it to the guard's mouth. He will quickly pass out. We then sneak up on the other guards and do the same."

"Why don't we just pistol whip them?"

"Because when they awaken, they would warn the other guards. If they just wake up from the chloroform, they'll just think they fell asleep and need to bathe to get rid of their body odor—it being the odor of chloroform."

"Wont they remember the attack?"

"Hopefully not, since chloroform has an amnesic effect. Even if they remember, the damage will already be done by the time they awake."

"And what will cause the damage?"

Max pulls out three large wolverine traps—with a smile.

At 3AM they arrived one hundred yards from the hacienda, hiding the horses in the trees, they placed a burlap bag over the horse's heads, to avoid them from warning the guards by whinnying or neighing. Walking with moccasins, they found only two guards sitting on the porch, leaning on a post and both sound asleep. Both were easily chloroformed into an anesthetic sleep.

Verifying that both front and rear doors were locked, the duo started checking all the windows to the porch. To their amazement, one window was not only unlocked but was obviously left open by accident. Stepping thru the window, they found themselves in an office. Max checked the desktop and verified it was the Marquis' office when he felt the hole left by Sylvia's Marlin nail. Two traps were set next to the door on what was likely a path to the office desk. The third trap was set and laid in front of the desk's chair, in case the first two traps failed to catch their prey. The duo departed and left the window open.

Arriving at their observation/shooting spot, the duo decided to stay alert in case some unplanned activity occurred. Wilbur asked what Max thought would likely occur.

"It all depends whether the Marquis enters his office in the dark, with or without a lantern, or enters in full daylight. If he spots our traps, our scheme will fail, and we'll have to try another route—plan B. If only one trap goes off, we'll hear the screaming from here, and that means we'll have a shot at him, today."

Meanwhile in the hacienda, the Marquis had awakened around 4:30AM. Lately he had intractable insomnia since his expulsion from San Antonio. He would drink cognac till he would fall asleep. Now awake this early, he reached for his cognac bottle but found it empty. Since his only supply was in his office, he would have to get up and get a fresh bottle.

The Marquis started down the stairway in the dark, walked thru the parlor, and headed to the office door. There was an usual smell in

> the parlor, but with the kitchen light on, he assumed the cook was starting breakfast. Using his keys, he unlocked the door and stepped inside. The cook heard two loud clicks as the traps went off. The scream that followed was enough to wake all the men in the bunkhouse. The cook ran to investigate, as she entered the office, she saw the Marquis' right foot in a trap and his right elbow in another trap. Both traps had pooling of blood and the Marquis was screaming at the top of his lungs, "get me out of this mess, now."

Meanwhile, some 500 yards away, Wilbur was dozing off as the howl from hell was clearly heard. Wilbur was startled and said, "what in blazes is that horrible sound?"

"That is music to my ears. The Marquis now knows he was lied to and realizes that I'm alive—and back to repay his kindness. Now it's showtime."

Meanwhile at the hacienda, the segundo and his men arrived on the scene. The Marquis was nearly unconscious, but when they released the traps, he was rudely awakened with more pain. Once he was laid on his back and pressure applied to the multiple lacerations from the toothed trap, the bleeding was controlled. The Marquis asked, "how could this breech of security have happened?"

The segundo reported. "The two guards were drugged with chloroform and the window to your office had been left open since there was no evidence of forced entry." The Marquis immediately realized that with his late evening cognac, that he was the one who left it open. Instead of admitting his error, he yelled, "it was the evening maid. Bring her to me, now."

As the maid arrived, the Marquis said, "look at what has happened to me because you forgot to lock this window." The maid looked shocked and said, "Senor, it was not I, since I was off and spent the day in town. As she was about to object even more, a shot ran out and the maid dropped dead. The Marquis, holding the smoking gun, added, "then maybe you should have been working instead of taking a day off."

The Marquis then ordered that a messenger be sent to get the local doctor to come and care for his wounds.

Meanwhile, the duo was on their feet and spotting with their 8X Malcolm telescopes. Suddenly, a rider left for town.

Max said, "as I suspected, he's sent for the local doctor. In forty minutes, the rider will return with the bad news—the doctor isn't coming. The patient will have to come to the doctor, heh?"

"How do you know he won't let his men take care of the wounds?"

"Because I smeared horse manure on the jaws and teeth. Without professional disinfectants, he will die of infection."

Meanwhile in the hacienda, the messenger returned with the bad news. The Marquis will need to ride to town. The discussion was held between the segundo and the Marquis. "you have enough experience dealing with wounds, you can care for my wounds."

> "No patron, these traps were contaminated with manure. You must have the lacerations disinfected with carbolic acid and then each one needs suturing. This must be done by the doctor."

> "Very well, wash my wounds, bandage them and prepare our trip come daylight. I guarantee you, once the doctor is done, that I will kill him for failing to come to my aid."

At the observation point, Max and Wilbur became alert when they saw the Marquis' carriage being harnessed. As it approached the hacienda's front door, it stopped in front of the door and steps. The duo recognized that their shot would need to be taken while the Marquis was on the porch. Once he descended to the carriage, the carriage would be in the way of their sight picture. That meant that they had at most a 5 to 10 second interval to reach their mark. Max said, "when the front door opens, get ready. When you hear me say, now, then fire your two shots at will."

As the door opened, Max saw two men nearly carrying the Marquis. Max said, "now." Two shots rang out followed by two more shots. Max saw the results in slow motion, after the fact. The Marquis obviously saw the rifle powder bloom as he mouthed—no! His body then jerked right and left followed by two strong pushes backwards onto the hacienda's front wall.

Wilbur confirmed the four direct hits. The duo started quickly to put their gear away and within minutes were galloping away from the shooting spot, leaving only evidence of horse tracks and manure. They stayed cross country for two solid hours till they had to stop to water and rest the horses. During that time, Wilbur asked, "what are the chances the segundo and his men will follow our tracks?"

"If you recall the pistol shot after the screaming, I suspect someone was killed for leaving the window open. Unless I'm mistaken, I think the segundo and his men are fed up of the abuse. I cannot believe that they would risk any more of their lives to salvage their patron's honor, since there is only dishonor and shame remaining."

"Yes, you're probably right. The segundo will likely bring the Marquis' body to the authorities, and Antonio Ramirez will take over after the investigation is complete."

Getting back on the cross-country trail, the duo continued for two hours at a medium trot, not to abuse their horses. Stopping every two hours for water and rest, they continued their escape till dark.

Just before stopping for the night, a Mexican sentry spotted the two "gringoes" and reported his findings to his boss. The boss was pleased, since Americans this far south usually meant a harvest of US funds for themselves. They made plans to invade their camp during the night and kill them both for what loot they could find, plus guns and horses.

When setting up camp, Max decided to take precautions. A full campfire was started to cook their hot meal of canned beef stew and coffee. After dinner, two false stuffed bedrolls were set up next to the fire pit. The last precaution was laying down a cord six inches off the ground and tied to cowbells. Max then opened his last large saddlebags and took out two double barrel shotguns—each with sawed-off barrels and stocks.

"Take this to the left of camp and I'll take mine to the right. If we get visitors tonight, it won't be a cordial visit. They will either be a Mexican posse out to hang us, or bandits who come to waylay us. Either way, they will all die—yes, shoot to kill."

Shortly after the duo went to their respective hideout, the Mexican gang started walking from their camp to the duo's camp. Around 2AM the cowbells started ringing followed by a barrage of gunfire at the fake bedrolls. Max yells out. "put your guns down or you're dead." As expected, the outlaws turned their guns towards the voice, which was hidden behind a huge pine tree. Wilbur let go both barrels as Max sneaked around the tree and also let go both barrels. After the smoke cleared, no one was left standing. All four Mexican bandits were dead.

Wilbur collected the guns and checked the dead men's pockets. They had a total of $279 US dollars. The guns were all new Winchester 73 and Colt 45's. Max said, "these outlaws have been attacking Americans before today. Let's walk back to their camp. We'll release their Mexican horses to the wild and check their saddlebags."

The horses were clearly large American geldings which could be used on the farm. The saddlebags had more US funds that added up to another $219. Max gave all the US funds totaling $498 to Wilbur and elected to keep the four large geldings and tack for the farm. The four pistols and four Win 73's would be kept as farm inventory.

Come morning the caravan took off for the US border. It was 3PM when they waded across the Rio Grande and made their way to town to report being waylaid by Mexican outlaws. Wes took down the information and made note of the different brands on the geldings. He said, "assuming no one asks for lost or stolen horses that match these brands, they are yours to keep. I will give you a legal bill of sale, to keep, in case you decide to sell them."

Wilbur stopped at the bank to make a deposit and then headed home. Max trailed the four horses to the homestead barn. He then snuck up to the greenhouse where Sylvia was watering the plants. When Sylvia spotted him, she ran into his arms and just held on without speaking.

It was Max who spoke first, "how is my beautiful wife and baby doing?"

"Much better, now that you're here. God did I miss you! Are you alright, is Wilbur Ok?"

After a significant pause, Max said, "now we can finally live in peace."

***

The business rolled on from season to season. The expansion of crop land had been along the road frontage that allowed the windmill water pump transfer to the roadside holding ponds. These ponds could irrigate downhill for at least five acres or +- 1000 feet. Now the cultivated plots covered the entire length of the two miles they owned along the river. Any expansion beyond the 1000 feet to the holding ponds would require a new method of bringing water to faraway cultivated plots.

Max saw the problem. Either they found a new method of filling distant holding ponds, or they had to buy more river frontage land and windmill pumps. Max went to town to the hardware store and spoke with Parker Caldwell. Once the problem was explained, Parker mentioned the solution. "Crop farming in South Texas is impossible without irrigation from the river. You're not the only one with the same problem. The hay farmers end up selling different grades of hay because some of their fields cannot get enough water. The solution is the new coal fired steam powered hydraulic pumps—just like the locomotive engines."

"Is this available on a private or industrial scale?"

"Both, there are now companies building huge plants, but small units are available for less than a thousand dollars. The specifications state that it can pump water up to three quarters of a mile and can fill enough holding ponds to irrigate two hundred acres."

"How long to get one here?"

"It will come in three pieces by train to Laredo, and then in three freight wagons via the water ferry. I can get one here in six to eight weeks. In preparation, build a one-foot thick concrete slab that measures 20X20 feet, next to the river, and centrally located over your new plots."

"Great, order one. It will take at least two months to dig four new holding ponds, cultivate the land and set up a downward slope with dikes for irrigation. By the way, any idea when the railroad will get to town?"

"Being on the town council, this is the latest and not to be repeated. We have a large ranching family that is donating large plots of land to make sure the railroad will not bypass this valley. There is also talk of eventually naming our town after the family name. Now the telegraph will be arriving in town in four months. That usually means the railroad arrives shortly thereafter. The nearest depot for you will be in town. Are you thinking of using the railroad to ship your produce afar?"

"Yes, we are."

"Then, I will start passing the word around to my salesmen. I bet you'll be getting inquiries directly at your homestead since your product is already getting east to Brownsville and west to Laredo."

Before leaving the store, Max saw a flyer advertising a machine to seal a tin can, how to process vegetables in tin cans instead of glass mason jars, and where to get a supply of pint and quart size tin cans. Max read everything, turned around and ordered the equipment and 1000 tin cans.

Getting home, Max explained everything to the family. The enthusiasm he generated was infectious. The game plan was to move ahead with all these changes. The first thing was to hire day workers and start digging holding ponds, irrigation ditches/dikes and leveling the cultivated lands. Later the concrete pad was built and sections of piping were purchased and laid out in ditches.

The canning market was extremely successful in the local market. The glass jars could be kept locally, but canned vegetables for distant markets would be in tin cans. This meant building a standing factory to sterilize, process and handle crates of vegetables. The old lean-to would be kept and modified to store empty tin cans.

The new factory was elevated, to allow for a loading dock for receiving wagons. Crates for transfer by train would be placed on wheeled platforms for easy loading to freight wagons and from freight wagons to railroad cars.

As things would sometimes occur on schedule, several business-men arrived to view the canning operation and possibly sign contracts. One such large distributor in Brownsville was fascinated with the canning process. Sylvia, nearly at term, gave the man a station by station tour of the facility: washing and rinsing cans, adding ripe vegetables covered with water, add a pinch of salt, place a cover and clamp into place, process to boiling temperatures, cooling station, label and company logo application, and crating. The business man saw the multiple labels to include: tomatoes, potatoes, carrots, string beans, beets, mixed vegetables and in the future cooked navy beans.

"Is there any vegetables you cannot preserve by canning?"

"No, I don't believe so, but I admit that certain vegetables retain their flavor better than others—and these are the ones we are canning."

"Well, I'm impressed. What is the shelf live for canned vegetables?"

"The shelf life for high acid foods like tomatoes is 18 months. For low acid vegetables, it's up to 4 years."

"Well, I'm convinced. My company, Texas Foods, distributes 10% of its product to Brownsville and 90% to all of Texas thru Houston. Sign with us and you'll have your product sold all over Texas within a year. The demand is here, and now is the time to strike, heh."

Max and Sylvia had a private meeting with the rest of the family and before the scout left the homestead, a one-year contract was in hand.

Things were moving along well till the barn-man suddenly passed away of old age. The hunt was on for a new barn-hand that was good with horses, could replace a shoe from a generic assortment, repair a harness, treat basic equine illnesses, and keep the two barns clean. Max had held interviews for two days and had yet come up with the right person. At the end of the second day a Comanche Indian applied for the job.

Max had the direct approach. "Tell me your name and your story why you want this job."

"My name is Soft Wind and my wife is called Red Flower. Our modern friends call us Breeze and Red. Life on the reservation is very difficult. We cannot accept charity like most of my tribesmen do. I want to work and earn my way. Now that our children have left the tribe, it is time for us to move along as well. My wife and I will work together as one person. She will be my helper, we'll live in a teepee next to the barn and prepare our own meals. We will work till the work is done. The hours do not matter. I love horses and can speak to them."

Max eyebrows went up. Red Flower saw his reaction and said, "Soft Wind can communicate with horses with a language of grunts and moans. You have to see it to believe."

"Ok, Breeze, show me your language. Breeze stepped to the corral, opened the gate, and started growling, grunting and moaning. To Max's surprise, all the horses' ears picked up and each one walked out of the corral to encircle Breeze. When the horses started neighing in response, Max couldn't believe his eyes. He then moaned and the horses went back to the barn to step in each of their own stalls.

Max asked them what they wanted for a salary. Breeze answered $1 a day for both. Max look at them and said, "I'll pay you as a team and give you $2.25 a day plus all the food you can use from the cook shack. Bring your horses, if you don't have any, you can use any horse and wagon in the barn. Glad to have you with us."

Red added, "I will also work in the field if you need me and thank you."

As the expansion project was under way,

Sylvia's time was also approaching. A week before her due date, Sylvia came home with news. Her visit with Doc Murphy included a surprise consultation with his new associate doctor by the name of Winston M Grapevine MD. Both doctors found it strange that the baby's head was not dropping into the birth canal. Dr. Grapevine postulated a cause but did not share it with Sylvia, he only shared his idea with Doc Murphy.

Within a week, Sylvia went into labor. Shortly after arriving at the hospital, her water broke, and her contractions picked up as expected. Both doctors kept listening to the baby's heart both during and in-between contractions. It was Doc Murphy who asked Doc Grapevine to explain what was going on.

"During each contraction, as the baby is pushed into the birth canal, the baby's heart slows down from a normal 140 bpm to an alarming 50 bpm. This is a sign of an entangled umbilical cord around the body or neck. It may also mean a very short cord from the placenta. This is unfortunately a set up for a damaged baby or a stillborn. We only have one recourse to avoid this tragedy—a C-Section with ether anesthesia, and both of us surgeons in attendance.

Sylvia looked at Max, and Max looked at Doc Murphy. Doc Murphy nodded with a look of absolute confidence. Max looked at Sylvia and she said, "What do you say, I need your help?"

"What do I know, all I want is you and our baby alive and well. This is your decision and I'll support whatever you decide."

"Without a single doubt. Let's do it. Life often requires us to take chances. This is one with the biggest personal pay off. Yes, I want a C-Section."

Doc Murphy simply whispered, "thank God you both have the wisdom of King Solomon!"

When Sylvia was wheeled to the operating room, the waiting room filled with the entire family, including Jenna's two-month-old baby boy. Outside the hospital were all the employees of **CIRCLE-C FOODS** and most of the town's merchants.

The surgery was immediately performed. When the uterus was opened, an extremely long umbilical cord was wrapped three times around the neck and once around the torso. A combination not compatible with a natural live birth.

Max was a total wreck. It was then that he realized that not knowing was just as bad as not being able to do anything about a problem. Suddenly the doors to surgery opened. Doc Murphy proudly announced that, thanks to Doc Grapevine, mother and child were both doing well. As soon as Sylvia is more awake and has fed your very hungry baby, we will call Max in."

As the doctors were leaving, Nellie asked, "was it a boy or girl?"

"That's up to the parents to announce."

Grant added, "boy that's not going to fly with that mob outside. Brian, will you go outside and talk to them?"

"No thanks, that's the big boss' job."

Max was finally called to Sylvia's room. As he entered, he saw his beautiful wife with the proudest appearance he had ever seen. Sylvia said, "come and see the most beautiful girl in the world, your daughter."

For a full week, the Adams' were a guest of Murphy's Valley Hospital. Max never left the room. Sylvia's recovery was uneventful and with the incision healing well, she was discharged. Once home, Max spent another two weeks bonding with his baby girl and serving Sylvia's every need.

At the end of the two weeks, Red Flower took

over assisting Sylvia so Max could get back to managing every day operations and the expansion project. Meanwhile, Sylvia found a name that would fit her daughter. She named her Jamie. When Max asked why she chose that name she said, "this baby is so alive and active, I suspect she'll be a tomboy. This neutral name will give her some leeway till she accepts womanhood."

And so, their lives were on solid footing. Max had put his bounty hunting years behind him, Sylvia had successfully started a profitable business and found the love of her life. The two together had been blessed with a healthy child and were on track to developing a statewide distribution for their canned produce.

***

EPILOGUE

Over the years, Sylvia gave birth to two boys, Jim and Justin. Running a statewide business and raising three kids required help. It was Red Flower who came to the rescue. All three kids loved her, especially tomboy Jamie, who followed her like an attached appendage. When puberty arrived, it was Sylvia who helped Jamie transition to womanhood. Over the formative years, Jamie became Sylvia's regular helper in the greenhouses. The boys were gladly added to the outside workforce.

All three children rode to school in town. After the 10th grade, they all went to some Texas college, accessible by train. Jamie became an accountant. Even with a busy practice in town, she came to the farm one day each week to make ledger entries and payroll. Jim went on to medical school and spent two years training in surgery. He returned to the hometown and became Doc Grapevine's associate when Doc Murphy retired. Justin went on to business school and always had every intention of returning to the farm. Everyone always knew that he would eventually become the farm's general manager.

It is of interest that all three children married original employee's children. Of note is Justin who married one of Wilbur's daughters—adding the Haggerton name to the Cassidy/Adams lineage. As Max and Sylvia approached retirement, they had seven grandchildren to spoil.

Sylvia was initially involved in planning and scheduling the farm's daily activities. With the expansion, two more greenhouses were added. From age 50, she spent all her time working in the greenhouses. She studied hybridization and succeeded in creating more hardy plants that also added taste to canned vegetables. Her other interests included soil analysis. She ordered the chemical agents and equipment to do her own analysis. With the new commercial fertilizers, she was able to replace the missing minerals. She even started checking the chemical content of composted horse and chicken manure— allowing the addition of deficient minerals and preventing the use of manure excessively high in ammonia from inadequate composting.

Max was totally committed to the expansion and the efficient farm's production. The town was growing in bounds when the railroad arrived. With the quick growth came more undesirables. Max had to occasionally help Wes and his deputies to arrest a criminal gang in town. Max was not keeping up his pistol skills, and always went to assist Wes with his sawed-off shotgun—the equalizer. By age 50, he had taken over the total control of the farm as Sylvia devoted all her time in the greenhouses.

Max also became know as a peaceful arbitrator. The Comanche's reservation was not getting enough food from the Indian agent. The beef supplies were adequate because of government contracts with local ranchers. But dry goods and vegetables were minimally available. Consequently, some braves were raiding nearby merchants and homesteaders, and stealing food staples other than beef. Max resolved the situation by allowing the Comanche to come to the farm once a week and pick up a full wagon of the vegetables that were needed. In addition, he made his benefactor fund available to provide the basics—flour, salt, oatmeal, baking powder, pepper, corn meal, sugar and coffee. When Jamie filed a complaint with the Indian Agency, the government, out of embarrassment, started paying the mercantile for the Indians needs and Max was also paid for one weekly wagon load of fresh vegetables.

Max recognized years ago that the farm's future rested on canning their produce. A new elevated plant was constructed with a loading dock. All modern equipment was added included a storage warehouse for the crated finished product ready for shipping. Canning produce was 95% of the farm's income. The plant's workforce included some thirty employees—about half of the farm's total workforce.

Grant and Nellie lived in the original homestead into their late- 80's. Since retirement, they enjoyed adding Justin and his family in the homestead house—along with two great grand-children. Justin's wife took over control of the household and was the senior Cassidys' helper and health provider till the end.

Max and Sylvia were able to see the growth of towns in the valley. For 100 miles, the Rio Grande Valley grew between Brownsville and Rio Grande City. The town to the west was finally name McAllen after one of the original ranching settlers. The community to the east, that Brian had serviced, became a combined community known as Weslaco/Donna. The original homestead became part of a new community called Alamo.

As Max, Sylvia, Brian and Jenna were approaching their 70's, retirement became the next step in their lives. After a short discussion of selling their farm home and moving into town, it was decided to stay on the farm. Like Brian and Jenna, Max and Sylvia continued attending their farmer's market—although Justin would send one of the workers as their assistant. All four of them were known to pinch in and help out when crunch days occurred. Brian's popular job was tilling, and Max's was working in the canning factory. Of course, Sylvia and Jenna preferred the greenhouses.

By the time Max and Sylvia passed, the **CIRCLE—C** logo was well known over Texas, New Mexico, Colorado, Oklahoma, and still growing. It was Max's famous line that became his epitaph—only in America can a determined couple leave an imprint on the business world.

***

THE END

Printed in the United States
By Bookmasters